The Book of Forgotten Angels

ANGEL RIVER
BOOK THREE

MISHA CREWS

Published by CWC Publishing

Because good books are essential for a happy life.

Cover design by Blue Water Books

Dear Reader,

Hello book buddies, and welcome to Angel River. (Or, if you've visited before, welcome back!) This is the third novel in the series, and the first book which does not revolve around Kate Doyle and Reed Fitzgerald, although they do have important parts to play in this story.

I have to admit, it was kind of fun to see Angel River through the eyes of Mae Wallace and Levi Morales, the central figures in this latest yarn. They are both relative newcomers to the town. Mae moved to Angel River in the early 2000s and bought the Angel River Café. Although she's become a fixture in the neighborhood, she's never really felt like she belonged. Then Levi arrives, in search of a rare novel. Levi is a good guy who's fallen a long way in his own estimation, and although he's trying to redeem himself, he definitely makes some mistakes along the way. Anyway, I'll let you get to know them on your own, through the pages of this book. I hope that you end up loving them as much as I do.

At the end of this novel is an Author's Note, which gives some background information about a few of the key characters and story elements. It also contains a hint or two about upcoming books in the Angel River series. I'll see you there!

Hugs and happy reading,

Misha

For all the book lovers, the read-past-your-bedtimers, the "just one more chapter" folks. You are my favorite kind of people.

"Be not inhospitable to strangers, lest they be angels in disguise."

George Whitman

PROLOGUE

ABEL STEIN, 1998

The book was small and featureless, almost insignificant. The brown fabric cover was worn, the corners frayed, and its compact shape did not take up much space on Abe's hotel dresser. Yet somehow, as he moved around the room, taking off his shoes, hanging up his jacket, the slim volume loomed very large in the corner of his vision.

Abe had spent the day surrounded by books, and now, at the end of many long hours, he didn't feel like reading. His plan was to order room service and see if he could find an old movie on television. But the book on his dresser called to him, seeming to fill the room with a gentle rumble, a sound akin to the low murmur of a dozen voices, or the rustle and sigh of wings.

When he could ignore the whispers no longer, Abe found himself settled on the bed, with his back propped up against pillows and the book in his hand. The table lamp was on, shade angled perfectly for reading.

Abe opened the cover, flipped past the frontispiece and the inscription, and found the beginning of the narrative. As his eyes traveled across the page, letters became words, words became thought. And before he knew it, he was transported out of his hotel room, and into the story.

The Book of Forgotten Angels
By Browning Weidler

First Bell

THE HAND THAT HOLDS THE PEN IS NOT TRULY IN CHARGE OF the words.

The same could be said for God and mankind. Womankind, of course, is a different story altogether, since she holds her own pen with such a ferocious grasp that surely even our Lord Himself must quake to attempt its direction. But further ruminations on that will have to wait for a different time.

I've begun my tale badly. Let me start again.

The story I am about to relate begins on Christmas Eve during Jonathan Strick's first year of mourning. His wife, I am sad to tell you, passed away on the first day of that very year, and poor Mr. Strick was left alone to care for their young daughter, Darla Louise.

Jonathan Strick was a writer, and was therefore naturally impoverished. At the time our tale begins, grief had cut the flow of his words until not even the tiniest drip of currency could be heard in the cavern of his pocket. But in December, an early gift had come his way in the form of a commission to write a story.

"Write a story that I can give to my wife on Christmas morning," his benefactor said, holding out a hand, which glinted with coin.

Jonathan took the money, seeing not its dollar value but

new shoes for his daughter and a meal for them both—something substantial enough to satisfy the pains of hunger instead of only mollifying them slightly.

His benefactor's hands slid back into his pockets, creating a musical jingle that promised further payment if Jonathan's tale pleased him.

"What should the story be about, sir?" Jonathan asked.

In response to the question, the man's lips twisted in a smile that was both sad and cynical.

"Angels," he replied.

CHAPTER 1

ANGEL RIVER, DECEMBER 2007

Mae

$\mathcal{A}$ s usual, Mae Wallace was at the Angel River Café by four thirty in the morning. The little restaurant didn't open until six, but Mae always gave herself plenty of time to prepare before she lit the neon sign that read *Coffee's On* and unlocked the front door to welcome the first customers of the day.

Mae parked in the small alley behind the building and entered through the back. She was welcomed by the warm scent of cinnamon, butter, and brown sugar. When she flipped on the light, she saw that the bakery racks were filled with tray upon tray of cranberry scones, croissants and muffins of every variety, as well as a dozen loaves of bread for toast and sandwiches.

Santa's elves had been hard at work. Or rather, one particular elf had been.

Four years earlier, when Mae had bought this café, she'd dreamed of spending her days covered in flour, kneading and mixing and glazing. She'd moved to Angel River from

Chicago, where she'd been a partner in a restaurant. For some reason, Mae had imagined that in a small town, she could spend the days with her hands buried in dough instead of with her head buried in a spreadsheet. She'd been wrong, unfortunately, and had eventually given over the delightful chore of baking to a nice young woman who lived locally. The girl liked to work nights. She came in around midnight, whipped up a batch of deliciousness, then was out the door again before anyone knew she was there. Mae consoled herself with the knowledge that the recipes were her own, so it wasn't like she was entirely absent from the creative process.

After Mae hung her coat and purse in the closet-sized room that served as an office, she washed her hands, donned her apron and turned on the espresso maker, ready to start the day with a latte and a slice of quiche. She would never trust a restaurateur who wouldn't eat their own food.

She had a quick bite to eat, then got to work turning on the grill, getting the chairs down from the tables, and making sure everything looked just right. The dining room was pleasantly festive, befitting the season. On every table there was a sprig of greenery in a tiny vase, tied with a small red bow. A lighted garland had been strung along the payment counter by the front door, and wreaths hung in both of the big glass windows. Mae loved the restaurant at this hour: dark and quiet and fragrant, waiting for customers to fill the booths and chairs. It was peaceful but exhilarating, like the last silent moments of predawn, right before the world wakes up and begins its day.

She had just filled the pastry case and double-checked the supply of sugar packets when someone knocked on the door. Not the front door, but the back door. Mae smiled and shook her head. They weren't expecting any deliveries, so that could only be one person: Donaghy, her cook. He was a

young man in his twenties, and he could be careless, sometimes. This wouldn't be the first time he had forgotten
his key.

With a teasing remark already hovering on her lips, Mae
made her way through the kitchen and unlatched the dead
bolt. She turned the knob and pulled open the door. But it
wasn't Donaghy who stood there waiting to come in from
out of the cold. It was a tall, dark, handsome stranger.

CHAPTER 2

*L*ater, Mae would chide herself for that description. *Tall, dark, handsome stranger. Really, lady?*

And yet, that was a precise characterization of the individual who stood on the other side of the threshold. The man was tall. The man was dark haired and handsome. And the man was a stranger to her.

He appeared to be about her age, which would put him in his early forties. Ordinarily, Mae might have been startled by the sight of any unknown person standing in front of her in the dark. But something about this man's was disarming. He looked too confused to be dangerous.

Still, she took the precaution of pulling the door closer to her body. When she spoke, it was with a guarded politeness. "Yes?"

The air was dry and cold, smelling of winter. The man crossed his arms over his chest, and his breath huffed out in a fog as he spoke.

"Good morning." His voice was pleasant, low, and somehow self-effacing. "I'm so sorry to be knocking on your door this early. I just got into town, and I figured someone might be here."

Mae waited.

He tried again. "I know this is odd, some stranger showing up on your doorstep. I'm looking for Mae Wallace. I understand she owns this place."

"I'm Mae," she said. "But we're not open for another hour or so."

The man's face had brightened when she'd confirmed her identity. Now it fell. "I'm sorry," he apologized again. "I'm on kind of a tight schedule, and like I said…"

"You just got into town. Yes, I heard you." Mae frowned. The man's diffident manner was starting to seem a little too forced. "We don't open for an hour and I—we have a lot to do before then. Can you come back?"

She'd changed "I" to "we" so it wouldn't seem like she was in the building by herself. It felt a little silly, but better silly than sorry.

He looked like he was going to ask one more time, and possibly apologize for the third time, when he relented. "Of course," he said. Then, as expected, "And I really am sorry if I startled you."

"It's okay." Mae gave a businesslike smile. "See you after six thirty."

The man fished a card from his pocket and held it out to Mae. His ungloved hands were well shaped, the nails clean and tidy. The hands were rough enough to make it obvious that he wasn't afraid of a hard day's work. And yet his fingers were long and elegant, appearing as sensitive as cat whiskers.

Mae reached out for the card, anticipating the instant when her skin would make contact with his. But at that moment, Donaghy arrived, breathless and flushed. He lived six blocks away and walked to work every morning. Actually, he often ran to work, because he was often late, and it looked as if this morning had been no different.

In spite of the fact that Mae didn't really think she was in any danger, she almost sighed with relief at the sight of him. Donaghy, a tall, slender young man, wasn't exactly an intimidating physical presence—especially not when he took off his knit cap and revealed hair that had been freshly dyed the color of a cranberry. But he was stronger than he looked, and at least Mae was no longer alone.

"Morning." Donaghy smiled a greeting at Mae then cast a blatantly curious look at the stranger on the doorstep. The man nodded slightly in greeting.

"Everything okay?" Donaghy asked.

"Absolutely." Mae returned his smile. "I'll be right in."

She opened the door a little wider, and Donaghy slipped past, disappearing into the kitchen.

The stranger was still holding out his card. Mae took it. The man backed up a few steps, sliding his hands into his pockets. He hesitated, as though waiting to see if Mae might change her mind and invite him to come in. When she didn't, he smiled slightly.

"I'll be back in an hour. Sorry, again, if I scared you." He turned and strode down the alley, his breath puffing on the cold morning air.

Mae closed the door and turned the lock. She held the card up to the light. It read "Levi Morales, Private Investigator." She pursed her lips, not sure what to think.

Donaghy came over, tying on his apron. "Who was that?"

Without a word, she handed him the business card. Donaghy's eyes widened. "Private investigator?" he drawled. "Ye gods and little fishes, that's exciting!"

Mae laughed out loud for the first time that day. She loved this kid. Ye gods and little fishes, indeed.

Donaghy was an interesting character. Not exactly the

kind of person one would picture as a whiz on the grill, but he could turn out fluffy eggs and tender sausage all day long. He had the ice-blue eyes of an Islandic fjord and the bone structure of a movie star. His real hair color was a luxurious, if unexciting, dark brown; the wild and ever-changing dye jobs were either a form of creative expression or young adult rebellion. Maybe it was a combination of the two. Or maybe it was just boredom. At any rate, Mae had a feeling that one day Donaghy would return to his natural hair color, put away the leopard-skin jackets and tight pants, and get a regular job. Or maybe not. In the meantime, she appreciated his expertise in burger flipping, and she loved having him around.

"I don't know about exciting," Mae said, in response to his comment. "But it certainly is different."

In spite of her words, she did feel a little pep in her step at the thought of seeing Levi Morales again. As she opened the shop to the first customers of the day, making coffee and exchanging holiday greetings, she watched to see when he would walk through the door.

It was six thirty on the nose when he crossed the threshold. Mae felt herself perk up as he found a table and pulled out a menu from behind the salt-and-pepper shakers.

She grabbed a fresh pot of coffee and crossed the dining room, refilling cups as she went. When she reached the table where Levi was sitting, she turned over one of the coffee cups and poured.

"Thank you," he said. "That smells great."

Up close and in the soft light of the café's overheads, Levi's face looked pale and tired. His eyes, brown with flecks of green, had dark circles under them. She wondered if he had indeed gotten into town at six o'clock that morning. If that was the case, where had he traveled from?

In response to his comment about the coffee, she asked, "Can I get you any food to go with it?"

He studied her seriously. "That depends," he said. "Will you sit and eat with me? My treat, of course."

"I can't sit long enough to eat, but I can get something started for you and then come back for a moment." When he didn't answer, she suggested, "How about eggs and bacon?"

He nodded. "Eggs and bacon it is."

It was a perfunctory order. Mae suspected that if she had suggested pancakes, or bratwurst, or pancakes with bratwurst, he would have said yes to that too. Whatever he was waiting to talk to her about, he apparently wasn't interested in much else.

As luck would have it, when she brought his food back to him, there was a lull in the shop. So, with a clear conscience, she sat down and poured herself a cup of coffee.

"Okay, Mr. Morales," she said. "What can I do for you?"

By that time, she thought she had figured out what his answer would be. Mae's ex-husband was a data analyst, and every time he started a new contract that required a security clearance, she got a phone call during which she was asked routine background questions. True, she'd never been visited by a PI before, but maybe this new job was just that much more intense.

Mae was completely astonished when Levi said, "I'm here to ask you about a book."

Reading the surprise on her face, he explained, "I have a client who collects first editions. He's interested in buying a copy of Browning Weidler's *Book of Forgotten Angels*. You're on the list of possible owners."

Mae blinked. "Browning Weidler?"

"He was a writer who lived in Angel River," Mr. Morales said patiently. "Not very well known but well loved by the few who have read his work."

Mae had heard the name, but she wasn't familiar with his work. "Why do you think I have his book?"

"The previous owner of your house bought the book at auction in 1983, but according to his attorney, it's not listed among the assets of his estate. I was told that it might have been left at the house when you moved in."

It was true that there had been a dozen boxes in the house when Mae had bought it. She'd put them into the shed, intending to go through them to see if she could find anything interesting. That had been an embarrassing number of years ago, and she'd all but forgotten about them until that moment.

Mr. Morales continued, "As I said, my client is interested in the book, and he's willing to pay. Do you have it?"

"I still have the boxes," she admitted. "I could look through and see if the book is in there."

"Great," he said. "I'll help you."

"I'm not sure that's a good idea." Mae was a trusting woman, but there was no way she was inviting a total stranger to her house so he could look through her things. At the very least, she had to find out a little bit about him.

Levi Morales opened his mouth as though he were about to argue, but Mae spoke first.

"Tell you what," she hedged. "I'm going to be working all day. But I'll call you later this afternoon and see what we can work out."

The man smiled briefly, sparking the green in his eyes. "And a few hours will give you some time to check me out. Okay, I respect that. If I don't hear from you by tomorrow morning, I'll come back around this same time. Fair enough?"

"Fair enough."

Mae stood, and Levi Morales did the same. He reached

into his pocket and pulled out cash, although he hadn't touched his food.

"Aren't you even going to stay and eat?" Mae asked. "I promise you, it's good."

He sank down slowly, almost grudgingly, and picked up his fork with a great show of politeness. Then he took a bite of the eggs, and color flooded into his cheeks. He began to eat enthusiastically.

Mae turned and headed back to the kitchen. "Enjoy your meal," she said over her shoulder, not caring if she sounded smug.

CHAPTER 3

*a*t midmorning, the flow of customers had slowed enough that Mae felt comfortable taking a break. She bundled up a basket of muffins and a cardboard thermos of coffee. Then she walked the five short but cold blocks to the Angel River Police Station.

A small foyer area served as a lobby. It held a few polished wood chairs and a front desk that always seemed to be empty. As soon as she was inside, Mae could hear a burble of voices. Her forward momentum slowed. Was she interrupting something important?

Through an archway, she could see the main office, which was divided into three workstations by desks set at angles to each other. At one of the desks sat the person she'd come to see: her friend Sharon, who was an officer in the police department. But Sharon wasn't alone at her desk. Also sitting there were Susie Fischer, who owned and ran the Angel River Hotel, and a woman who Mae recognized as Kate Doyle, who was somewhat famous around town.

Kate had grown up in Angel River and had recently moved back, along with her new husband, Reed Fitzgerald, who was also a town native. The pair had become local celebrities, of a sort. Reed had been a wealthy businessman in New York and had become a town benefactor, spreading his prosperity liberally to various needy causes. Kate was a lawyer and was four months pregnant with the couple's first child.

The three women were clustered around Sharon's desk. Mae had walked in on them mid laugh, heads thrown back, teeth flashing. Although it was a cheery sight, it gave Mae a slightly cold, alien feeling, as if she were the only girl at school who hadn't been invited to the party. She shook off the mood and forced a smile.

"Morning, ladies," she called from the archway.

Her appearance was met with exclamations of happy greeting. Sharon stood up and came over to Mae, drawing her forward into the group and pulling up a chair for her. Mae appreciated the gesture, but she couldn't help feeling like an average duck among gilded swans. Her brown hair was unremarkable, and her figure inclined toward round-ness. She got a lot of exercise, but she was too fond of her own cooking to maintain the svelteness of her youth.

On the other hand, Kate was petite and polished, with delicate features and golden eyes set off by lush auburn hair. Susie was tall and slender, with a sunny smile and deep, engaging dimples. And Sharon—well, Sharon was a bombshell. There was no other word to describe her. Tall, blonde and beautiful. Her manner was restrained but friendly to the people who she liked, restrained and down-right rude to those she didn't. But she had a good heart, and as an officer she was a professional first, last, and always. She nodded at the basket of goodies that Mae carried.

"I can tell by your expression that you're here to ask for a favor," she said. "And those muffins look so good that I'm ready to say yes to just about anything. Plus, I'm starving, so that doesn't hurt your cause. Come have a seat."

Susie had already stood up to grab coffee mugs from a nearby counter. "So great to see you," she told Mae. "Feels like it's been weeks."

"It's a busy season," Mae replied easily. "I bet the hotel has been packed."

"And then some," Susie agreed. "I thought business would drop off after Thanksgiving weekend, but we're still full."

Mae was glad to hear it. Little towns like Angel River, with no specific industry of their own, relied on tourism to keep the economy going. That was especially true of a hotel, of course. Her business at the café was always brisk, but she was lucky.

She noticed that Kate didn't reach for the coffee. "Sorry. I didn't think to bring decaf," Mae said apologetically.

"Oh, don't apologize," Kate replied hurriedly. "You had no way to know that I'd be here. Besides," she dropped a hand to her stomach, "this little girl isn't too fond of coffee. Even decaf gives me an upset stomach."

"You're having a girl?"

Kate nodded, a pleased smile breaking over her face. "Reed is over the moon."

"I'll bet." If Mae had been a little more self-confident, she might have hugged Kate. But the women didn't know each other that well, and Mae didn't want to overstep. Instead, she held the basket in Kate's direction. "Would your little girl like one of these?"

"Oooh, carrot," Kate murmured, taking a moist muffin off the top. "I accept on behalf of both of us."

"Carrot cake counts as vegetables," Susie told her earnestly.

"I couldn't agree more," Kate replied.

As Mae took a seat across and reached for her own mug

of coffee, Sharon explained that the women had met to discuss the idea of holding a Fall Festival during the following year.

"I remember there was one the first year I came to town," Susie said. "I thought it would be fun to resurrect it."

She had brought the idea up to Kate, and then they had decided to run it by Sharon to see what kind of security—if any—they were likely to need.

Mae slipped her hand into her coat pocket and fingered Levi's card. She had hoped that Sharon would help her find out something about him, and of course she'd had no way to know that the other two ladies would be here. Was this the kind of thing she wanted to bring up in public? She hadn't told anyone else about it yet, not even Trina, who was her assistant manager and close friend.

Sharon, unaware of Mae's dilemma, selected a bran muffin for herself. She put it on a napkin and popped the top off to eat later. "Saving the best for last," she murmured. Then she pulled off a section of the bottom and put it into her mouth, closing her eyes as she savored. "Perfect," she said.

She opened her eyes again and said, "Okay, coffee temptress, what can I do for you?"

Mae couldn't help but laugh. "I like the idea of being a coffee temptress. I think I'll adopt it as my official job title."

Hesitantly, she pulled out Levi's card. She held on to it for a moment, trying to decide whether she should come back when Sharon was alone. Kate must have sensed her discomfort because she asked, "Would you like some privacy? Susie and I can step out."

"Oh no, that's all right," Mae said. There was no way she was asking a pregnant woman to wait in the lobby, even for the few minutes it might take to have this conversation.

Besides, this was a small town, and word of Levi's visit was bound to get out, so Mae might as well spill it now.

In a few short sentences, she told the women what had happened that morning, and why she was there. She held the card out to Sharon, who took it. "Is there any way you can check this guy out for me?"

Sharon pulled back slightly, glancing at Susie and Kate. "I can't use the official database for anything personal." She examined the card. "But on my lunch break, I can do some digging into social media and other places. I can at least verify that his PI license is valid. That's public info. I'll cast my professional eye on it, and if I see anything fishy, I'll let you know."

"I appreciate it," Mae said. "Thanks so much."

"You say he wants a book?" Kate asked.

Mae nodded. "By someone named Browning Weidler. I had never heard of him before this morning."

Susie said she'd never heard of him, either. But Kate and Sharon, who had been born in Angel River, nodded immediately.

Sharon said, "All of us local kids learned about him in English class. He published a few stories after the Civil War, right?" She looked at Kate.

"That's how I remember it," Kate agreed. "He never got famous outside of town, but there used to be a display about him at the library, and I think that at one point, they were planning some sort of statue for him in the town green."

Mae fiddled with her coffee cup. "Well, if this offer is valid, it would be nice."

With typical bluntness, Sharon asked, "How much did he say his client wants to pay for the book?"

Mae felt herself flush at the mention of money, but she answered honestly. "He didn't mention an exact figure."

"Mm-hmm," Sharon pursed her lips. "If you find the

book, get something in writing before you turn it over to him."

"Good idea. I should have thought of that, myself." Mae's cheeks warmed with embarrassment. Was she a business-woman, or wasn't she?

"The best ideas always come after the fact," Sharon said kindly. "I probably wouldn't have thought of it at the time, either."

"Thanks." Mae smiled ruefully, then took a deep breath. Time to get back to real life. "I should let you ladies get back to your meeting."

"Oh, do you have to go?" Susie asked. "I was hoping you might stay and help us talk over this Fall Festival thing. It's going to be a huge project to pull off."

Mae had started to stand and gather her things. "Sure." She settled back in her chair. "I can stay awhile."

SHE RETURNED TO THE CAFÉ JUST AS THE EARLY LUNCH CROWD was beginning to gather. The rush of customers kept her mind off Levi Morales and the intriguing possibilities of his presence in town.

Shortly before two o'clock, Mae got a call from Sharon who, true to her word, had spent her lunch hour digging into the legitimacy of what Levi had told Mae that morning.

Customer traffic had hit a lull, so Mae was in her tiny office, catching up on some bookkeeping. When she heard Sharon's voice on the line, she reached out and eased the office door shut for privacy.

"What did you find out?" Mae asked.

"There's good news and possibly bad news." Sharon's voice had a slight echo, and the engine hum in the back-ground told Mae that the officer was driving.

Mae leaned back in her chair. At the mention of bad news, her heart sank. "Which do I want to hear first?"

"Well, the good news is that the guy appears to be legitimate. His PI license number checks out, and his pictures on social media match the description you gave me. The only off-putting thing that I found was a Wyoming arrest back in '98, but the charges were dismissed."

"Arrest?" Mae sat forward again. "What for?"

"The charge was aggravated assault."

"Oh my God." A vision of Levi's elegant hands rose in Mae's mind.

"Don't freak out," Sharon said. "I don't want to minimize whatever might have happened, but like I said, the charges were dismissed. It's entirely possible that he didn't actually commit the crime."

In spite of her worry, Mae's lips curled into a smile. "You're a cop. Aren't you supposed to assume that everyone's guilty?"

"Some charges are completely bogus." Sharon's voice was grim. "And it's because I'm a cop that I know that."

Mae waited a beat, to see if Sharon would say more. When she didn't, Mae asked, "So what do I do, here?"

"I've got a call in to the county clerk," Sharon told her. "Court documents are public records, so I should have details for you by this afternoon. In the meantime, just exercise common sense. Let me know when he's going to be out at your place, and I'll come too. I get off at five today, so I can be there any time after that."

"Thanks, Sharon," Mae said warmly. "I really appreciate it."

"Of course. That's what friends are for."

Mae heard Sharon's turn signal clicking. There was the sound of tires crunching on gravel, the burr of the emergency brake, and then the engine went silent.

Sharon said, "Text me when you have an appointment with Levi, okay? I'm out at Wendell Beaufort's place for a wellness check."

Wendell Beaufort was a bit of a hermit. He lived outside of town on an unusual property which was known as the Twin Sisters. Mae had heard a lot about it but had never been there. Wendell only came to town every couple of weeks.

"It's good of you to check up on him."

Sharon brushed off the compliment. "Part of the job."

"Don't sell yourself short," Mae said. "You have a kind heart."

"More like a soft heart. With a soft head to match." Sharon chuckled. "He's a funny old guy. I like spending time with him."

"Well give him my regards, and let him know he can come by any time for a meal, free of charge." Nobody in town would go hungry if Mae could help it.

When she and Sharon had ended their call, Mae scrolled through her phone until she found Levi's contact information, which she had saved before she'd given his card to Sharon. Mae was about to call him when she remembered her decision to keep their communication in writing. She set the phone down and pulled her keyboard over so she could send him an email.

In the message, she gave him her address and said she could meet him at her house at five thirty. She made a point of reiterating that she wasn't at all sure the book was in her possession, but that if it was, she would want a written contract before turning it over. After some cogitation, she added, "Not to sound overly mercenary, but I would appreciate knowing how much your client expects to pay for the book if we do find it."

With that out of the way, she tried to forget about the

matter and focus on the rest of her day. Outside, the sky grew cloudy, as if snow might be on the horizon, but Mae had lived in this town long enough to know that those colors were just a tease. Angel River probably wouldn't see snow until February, although a few years previous, they'd had a doozy of a storm on Martin Luther King Day.

It was Friday, which meant that the café would be open until nine. At four o'clock, Trina, the assistant manager, arrived, followed by their dinner cook and two part-time servers. Leaving the café in these capable hands, Mae headed out to her car.

Before she pulled out, she checked her Blackberry and saw that Levi had replied to her email. His message was simple, but it made her breath catch.

Client willing to pay 25k. Thanks for the address. See you at five-thirty.

Twenty-five thousand dollars? For a *book*? A book that she might have in her *house*?

Mae sat, stunned, thinking about the things she could do with that money. It wasn't a fortune, but still… there could be nice Christmas bonuses for her employees, to start. A donation to the local foodbank. Maybe even a down payment on a new grill.

She texted the appointment time to Sharon, then started the car. The engine flared to life. "Okay, Browning Weidler," she murmured. "Let's go find your book."

MAE ARRIVED HOME WITH A FAMILIAR SENSE OF PEACEFUL satisfaction. The house was essentially an elongated log cabin, with a porch running the full length of the front. Long and low-slung, the building hugged tightly to the earth, giving the impression that the logs were still clinging to the soil from which they'd grown.

Beside the cabin and across a little courtyard, on the other side of a small garden that was bedded down for winter, was the barn. Mae still couldn't believe that she, a city girl all her life, owned a real barn: tall and broad, with red-painted sides and wide doors. A seven-pointed star, traditional in this part of Virginia, highlighted the peak of the dark-green roof. Out of sight, tucked into a far corner of the garden, was the shed where she thought she might find her buried treasure.

As Mae crossed her front yard, the name of the man who had owned the house materialized in her mind. Abel Stein—that was it. How could she have forgotten a name like that? He'd built the cabin in the early seventies and had lived in it for the rest of his life. Mae had moved to Angel River in the early 2000s and had bought the place immediately. In between, it had stood vacant, empty except for the boxes of books that she'd stored in the shed. And today, for the first time, she would open them and see what was inside.

She climbed the wide front steps, opened the front door, and walk in. There, perched expectantly at the edge of the entryway rug, was Ruby. The cat was a small blue point Siamese, with delicate fur gently shaded in soft, elegant gray and intelligent eyes the color of clear, perfect sapphires. As soon as Mae entered, Ruby stood and howled imperiously.

"I know, your majesty," Mae sighed. "You're hungry. You're starving and neglected. I get it."

As Mae closed the door, Ruby came forward and circled Mae's legs. The cat allowed herself to be stroked briefly, then she hastened toward the kitchen, leading the way with her tail held high. Mae followed obediently.

In the kitchen, Mae picked up Ruby's bowls from that morning, dished fresh food and water into clean bowls, and set them down in front of her impatient mistress. When the cat hunkered down to eat, Mae realized that she hadn't even taken off her coat yet. She laughed and shook her head at her own folly. In this house, the cat's needs always came first.

She returned to the foyer and had just hung her coat in the closet when the doorbell rang. Well, that was good timing. She glanced at her watch. It was just before five o'clock. Sharon must be early.

Mae opened the door, a greeting for her friend hovering on her lips. But it wasn't Sharon. It was Levi.

"I'm early," he said apologetically. "I got here faster than I expected. And, hello."

"Hello." Mae's reply was automatic. She hesitated, wondering whether she should let him in while she was alone in the house. *Aggravated assault,* Sharon had said. That was serious stuff.

She looked up into his green-flecked eyes, and her heart gave a little leap that had nothing to do with fear. The truth was, she was attracted to this man, and maybe even a little fascinated by him. Levi was handsome, age appropriate, and engaged in an interesting profession. All of those things made her want to get to know him better, and that feeling worried her. Romantic notions had a tendency to cloud one's judgement.

"I could come back in thirty minutes," Levi offered. "Did I catch you in the middle of something?"

"No." Annoyed by her own indecisiveness, Mae stepped back and opened the door for him. "I'm sorry, Mr. Morales, I was woolgathering. When you rang the bell, I thought you were my friend Sharon. She's coming to lend a hand, and she'll be here in a few minutes."

Mae added, "Don't be surprised if she's in uniform when she arrives. She's a police officer."

He gave her an understanding smile as he stepped over the threshold. "Call me Levi," he said. "And thank you."

She hung his coat in the closet. The tan of his sheepskin

looked good next to the dark green of her wool overcoat. They almost seemed to belong together. Pushing away that fanciful thought, Mae turned around, and she practically bumped into him. He took a quick, inelegant step backward.

"Oops. Small foyer. Would you like some coffee?" she asked, to cover the awkwardness of the moment.

His eyes lit up. "Is it the same brew you serve in your café?"

Mae couldn't help but smile. "As a matter of fact, it is."

"Then the answer is definitely yes."

"Come on into the kitchen." She turned and led the way through the living room. Levi's footsteps slowed as they passed the wall of built-in bookshelves. Although Mae didn't turn to look at him, she could picture his eyes scanning the volumes on the off chance that what he was looking for was already in plain sight.

"Those are mine," she said over her shoulder, "and they're mostly mysteries, some romance and thrillers, too. Not very literary, but I love them, and I like to keep them and revisit the worlds from time to time."

"I get that," Levi said. "I like mysteries too. To be honest, I've never had much use for classics like this Weidler book. But some people are obsessed with them. I've never tracked down a rare book before, so this is kind of new territory for me. It's fun, though."

"I imagine it would be."

She had kept moving as they talked, and he followed her around the corner and into the kitchen. She motioned for him to have a seat, and he did, pulling out one of the two chairs at the small kitchen table.

Ruby came over and sniffed him, graciously allowing her head to be rubbed. Then she did the unthinkable and jumped right up onto the table, flopped over, and allowed Levi to pet her belly.

Mae stared in astonishment. "You must be a cat person," she said. "I've hardly ever seen her be that friendly that fast with anyone."

He stroked the cat's silky fur. "I do enjoy the company of felines," he said. "I lost my tabby, Gregory, to leukemia, and I haven't been the same since. Haven't been able to bring myself to get another cat either."

"I completely understand." Mae started the coffee brewing. As the homey aroma filled the kitchen, she heard herself say, "Ruby was my mother's cat. Mom passed away a few years ago, and Ruby and I have been consoling each other ever since."

The moment of self-revelation surprised her. It wasn't like her to confide in strangers. Suddenly agitated, she reached out and rubbed the cat between the ears. Ruby's eyes slitted with pleasure.

For a second, Mae had been afraid that Levi was going to offer condolences on her loss, which would somehow make the moment more difficult. When he sat silent, she felt heartened enough to add, "Of course, I worship Ruby, and she merely tolerates me, but we make it work."

"Such is the way with cat people," Levi replied simply.

Mae turned back to the coffeepot and reached for some cups. "So true."

CHAPTER 4

*T*he coffee tasted just as good as Levi remembered from that morning. It was even better, actually, as he was drinking it out of one of Mae's personal mugs, which were wide-mouthed and painted with daffodils.

Levi liked everything about the small, comfortable kitchen. The table at which he sat was round and scrubbed clean, with a neat pile of napkins in the middle next to cow-shaped salt-and-pepper shakers. The sink was tucked under the window. Pots hung from a rack over the stove, and an old cabinet with blue and white dishes was on one side of the room. Not an inch of space was wasted, and Levi appreciated that. He was from Wyoming. He liked open space outside and coziness in. Mae's kitchen was all kinds of cozy.

He liked Mae too. When she'd hung their coats side by side, he thought they looked like a good pair. But that was a whimsical notion, almost juvenile, and he was a grown man who was here for business. Nothing more, nothing less.

Still, it was tricky for him to sit there and try to make intelligent conversation while Mae's blue eyes rested casually on his face and her soft brown hair brushed her shoulders when she tilted her head ever so slightly. Everything about her was warm and restful—a little too perfect for his comfort.

Despite his interest in her, Levi was no good at small talk, and Mae's mention of her mother had nearly elicited a confidence that Levi wasn't quite ready to share with anyone. Even his own sister didn't completely understand why he was here. She'd been angry when he left "haring off after some old book," and he had not been able to bring himself to explain his actions.

It would all make sense when he returned home, he'd told her. But had it been his sister Ruth he'd wanted to convince —or himself?

Mae's front doorbell rang, saving him from having to make polite chitchat.

"That's Sharon. Be right back." Mae stepped out and returned with a movie star dressed as a police officer. It took a split second for Levi to realize that the woman standing next to Mae actually *was* a police officer. She was tall and shapely and had the finely made features of someone who should have been destined for a life in the spotlight.

Sharon was carrying a duffel, which she set on the ground as she accepted a cup of coffee from Mae. She nodded to Levi as Mae introduced them, studying him with the detached, somber eyes of law enforcement.

"Mae tells me you're looking for a book by Browning Weidler."

"That's right." Levi sipped his beverage and accepted her scrutiny. He thought he knew what was coming.

"I grew up around here, so I learned about him in grade school," Sharon continued. "I didn't know his books were considered valuable."

"Everything is valuable to someone," Levi replied. "But you're right. There isn't a huge market for his books. First editions are rare, though, because there weren't many of his books published. At least, that's what I've been able to glean from the research I've done."

"That makes sense," Sharon said. "And your client is eager to get his hands on this book in particular?"

"It was Weidler's only Christmas novel," Levi explained smoothly. "The man I'm working for would very much like to have it before Christmas."

Sharon seemed to digest his answers as she drank her coffee. Levi glanced at Mae and saw that she was leaning against the sink, watching the exchange. He smiled faintly, understanding the situation better than they could have imagined.

Mae caught his eye, and their gazes locked. His pulse jumped, and he tried to look away but found that he couldn't. Mae's lips parted slightly, and Levi leaned forward. It was as though the distance between them had suddenly evaporated.

Finally, Mae tore her eyes away from his, and she blurted, "Sharon, why don't you just ask him?"

Physically shaken by that brief moment, Levi gripped the cup in his hands. He needed something to hold on to. He inhaled through his nose, and out through his mouth. What he truly needed was to get past this awkward subject and get into those boxes of books. "Let me guess. You found out that I was arrested a few years ago and you want to make sure that my intentions are pure?"

It was the right thing to say, apparently, because both of them laughed. He hadn't really meant it as a joke, but that was okay.

Sharon was the one to reply. "Something like that. We know that the charges against you were dismissed, but I wasn't able to get as many details from the county clerk as I would have liked."

Levi nodded and pursed his lips. Then he shrugged. He

had nothing to lose by telling the truth, at least about this. He spoke flatly. "My wife was having an affair. I got into a fight with her boyfriend. I was arrested and charged with assault. The man declined to press charges, and the county decided not to prosecute. I'm still ashamed of my actions, and I know how lucky I am not to be in prison right now." That last part was especially true.

"Wow," Mae murmured.

Levi risked another glance at her and saw that she was staring meditatively into her coffee cup. Ruby, who was still on the table, batted his hand with her paw, and he rubbed behind her ears. For a long moment, her purring was the only sound in the room.

Then Mae spoke, her soft voice cutting briskly through the awkwardness. "Thank you for your honesty, and I'm sorry you had to go through that experience. Would either of you like a refill on your coffee, or are you ready to tackle the storage shed?"

Sharon gave Mae an intent look, which Mae returned calmly. Although Levi had only met them both today, he could plainly read Mae's expression. *Let's get this show on the road.*

Finally, Sharon said, "I'm ready if you are." She set down her cup and picked up her duffel. "Do you mind if I use your bedroom to change out of my uniform?"

"Of course," Mae said. "You know where it is."

Suddenly, Levi realized that he didn't want to be left alone with Mae. Given his current state, he didn't trust his emotions, and she was the type of woman who would likely bring those out. He stood, and asked, "Where's your restroom?"

She directed him to it. By the time he returned to the kitchen, Sharon was also back, and had changed into jeans and a sweatshirt. Mae assured them that the storage shed was heated, so they decided to leave their coats inside. She took them out the kitchen door into the little garden, leading them around a narrow path to a storage shed that had been tucked out of sight.

Mae unlocked the padlock, but before she opened the door, she turned to them and gave a sideways grin. "You're about to see my biggest embarrassment. Please don't judge me."

"Never," Sharon replied, in the voice of a stout and devoted friend.

Mae pulled open the door, reached in, and flicked on a light. Levi, not wanting to appear too eager but also not fully able to restrain himself, stepped forward and peered over her shoulder.

The interior was small and crowded with boxes of every shape and size. Although the volume of stuff made his heart sink a little, the dry warm air that filled the space buoyed his spirits back up again. The book, if it was there, could very well be in good condition.

"I know I should have gotten rid of all this years ago when I moved in," Mae said. "But I haven't had time to go through it properly, and I also haven't had the heart to just throw it away without at least looking to see what's here, you know?"

"I do know." Levi would have done the same, in her position. These boxes could be a treasure trove. "Are you sure you don't mind helping me go through them?"

He caught a sideways glance from Sharon, and realized that it was a stupid question. They wouldn't trust a stranger to dig through these things. Nor should they. But Mae's reply was tactful. "It's more like you're helping me by giving me a chance to see what's here. Then I can finally get rid of anything that I don't want. Besides," she added, "many hands make light work."

"Very true." The saying touched his heart. It was one of his mother's favorites.

They set up three folding chairs and quickly fell into a routine. Levi unpacked the boxes a little at a time. Mae made a careful list of everything. Sharon repacked after Mae had made her inventory notes.

Outside, the late afternoon slipped into evening, which was then overtaken by night. The temperature dropped, and the wind picked up. Inside the shed, they were cozy and surrounded by books, which was more pleasant than Levi had thought possible. When they took a quick break, Mae made a thermos of coffee and brought out some sandwiches so they could eat as they worked. Mae and Sharon talked in spurts, discussing the goings-on in town. There was a festival being planned for next year which sounded like fun. Several times they tried to pull Levi into the conversation, but he had retired into himself as he focused on the task at hand. It was an old habit with him, one which had driven his ex-wife crazy. For Mae and Sharon, he tried to balance politeness with his natural inclination for silence, but soon they gave him up as a hopeless cause, which was exactly what he was.

It took them until almost nine o'clock to go through all the boxes. In the end, Levi had to admit the truth: although the boxes proved to be full of many interesting volumes, *The Book of Forgotten Angels* was not one of them.

He leaned back, feeling grimy and chagrined. He had been so sure that his prize would be there. It just made sense. As he'd told Mae, Abel Stein had bought the book. There was no record of him selling it, and it wasn't on his estate inventory. Logically, then, it should have been in one of these boxes.

Unless he'd given it away. Or sold it without recording the sale. Or lost it, or burned it, or….

Suddenly, Levi was aware that he had been awake for

almost thirty hours. He had left Hepner, Wyoming, the night before last, and had driven as far as he could before he stopped at a motel and collapsed on a lumpy bed. His sleep had been fitful, his adrenaline still pumping. He'd risen at dawn and driven onward, not stopping until he arrived at Mae's café. That afternoon in his motel, he'd tried to nap but hadn't quite made it. Now exhaustion cracked down on him like a steel trap, and he knew he wouldn't be able to function until he got some good sleep.

He stood slowly, hearing a creaking in his joints that would not have been there a few years ago.

Getting old and rusty, he thought. *Not to mention useless.*

He felt Mae's gaze on him and turned to see her regarding him with sympathy.

She spoke quietly. "You're exhausted and disappointed, aren't you? I'm sorry, Mr. Morales. I really thought the book would be here."

He forced a smile. Mae was a nice woman. She didn't need to be subjected to his moods and regrets. "Are we back to 'Mr. Morales' again? I thought you were going to call me Levi."

She didn't answer. She just stood there, looking at him with soft understanding. Unexpectedly, Levi felt the crimp of tears behind his eyes and spoke briskly, "Well, I certainly appreciate your assistance and company—both of you," he added, including Sharon with a smile.

Remembering what he'd told her about the money, he said to Mae, "I'm sorry if I got your financial hopes up. You're the kind of person who deserves a nice windfall."

She shrugged. "Don't worry about that. I won't miss what I don't have. And I did find some books that I'd like to keep for myself."

Mae indicated a stack of a dozen or so books that she'd set aside to bring into the house, ranging from a book on birds to a trio of Ian Fleming novels to a collection of Fitzgerald short stories.

"Abel Stein had certainly possessed a variety of reading matter." Levi tried not to sound bitter that the book he sought wasn't among them.

"That he did," Mae agreed. "What are you going to do next?"

That was the question, wasn't it?

CHAPTER 5

ABEL STEIN, 1998

*A*be had never considered himself much use to God or man. But all that changed the day he first laid eyes on *The Book of Forgotten Angels*.

And to think that he'd almost walked right by it.

The book rested under a glass countertop. It was small and unassuming, covered in brown fabric. There was no dust jacket, no fancy engraving. It was an ugly duckling amongst literary swans. Abe glanced its way, his eyes skipped across the book's surface, and he continued forward, not even thinking twice.

Not, that is, until it whispered to him.

Abe stopped in his tracks, wondering if he had been mistaken. He closed his eyes and held his breath, and then it came again: that soft murmur, wordless yet eloquent.

Without another thought, he turned and walked back to the counter.

As he studied the homely little volume, wondering why it had called him, a young woman approached. When she was close enough for him to see her clearly, he realized that she wasn't as young as she'd appeared from a distance. There were sharp creases between her nose and mouth, and her dark, curly hair was run through with silver. But her forehead was smooth and high, and her eyes, though lined, were round and full of bright anticipation: an expression that matched the name on her tag, which read "Hope."

"Can I help you?" the woman asked.

He told her what he wanted to see, and her face lit up.

"It's a lovely book," she said, sliding on a pair of white cotton gloves. "This copy is signed by the author."

He thought the word "lovely" was overstating it a little but didn't bother voicing that opinion. She brought the book out and laid it on the counter. When she opened the front cover, the scent wafted up: paper and old ink, with hints of dampness and dirt. His heart swelled. It was a kind of magic, that smell. An elixir to cure all ills. It was the perfume of story.

Then Hope turned to the title page, and Abe saw the inscription written in the author's hand.

"To a young man with a bright future," Abe read out loud. "May it come sooner rather than later. Signed, Browning Weidler."

Entranced and mystified, he looked up into Hope's vivid eyes. "What does it mean?" he asked.

"That's a mystery," she said with a sympathetic smile on her face. "Just like the author himself. We don't have any pictures of him, no records of when he was born, or who his family was. We know he was from a little town in Virginia called Angel River, but—"

"Angel River?" Abe asked, startled. Then he began to laugh. It made sense now. He knew why the book had whispered to him, why it had beckoned him from two dozen feet away to come closer and take a better look. And more than that, he knew what it was telling him.

Hope smiled uncertainly, as if she wanted to join in his

mirth but wasn't sure she should commit herself to merriment. "What's so funny?" she asked.

"It's true what they say," he replied. "You can leave your home, but it never really leaves you."

And then he told her his story.

HOPE LISTENED, NODDING SYMPATHETICALLY AT INTERVALS, unsurprised by anything he said. His narrative was a common one, after all. He'd been born in a small town, had fallen in love with a girl who hadn't loved him back. When she had run off to Haight-Ashbury, he'd joined the Army. He'd survived the nightmare of Vietnam, expecting to die every moment of his tour. When he'd found himself back in the United States, he could not bear the thought of going back to Angel River. And so he hadn't.

He'd gotten a job that had made him a little money. And he'd learned the trick of turning that money into more money.

"And since I don't have children or close family to speak of," he finished, "I collect books."

Hope smiled rather sadly. "It's a good thing to do." She touched the volume in front of her. "This book means a lot to me. It's my personal copy. I never thought I would sell it, but, well…" She lifted her chin and said the last words with as much dignity as she could muster, "family troubles."

Abel held up a hand. "Say no more. Just because I don't have a family doesn't mean I don't understand trouble." He reached into his back pocket and pulled out his wallet. "How much are you asking for it?"

She named a sum and held her breath. The man in front of her—whose name she now knew was Abel Stein—seemed like a good sort of person. But when it came to matters of money, concepts of goodness tended to blur.

Without a word, Abel pulled out a sheaf of bills. He counted them, folded them in half, and pressed them into her palm. It was twice what she'd asked for.

She objected, but only half-heartedly, because she truly did need the money. When he insisted that she take it, she tucked the bills into the cashbox with trembling fingers.

Hope wrapped her beloved book carefully in brown paper, tying it with twine. She had to swallow a sob as she held it out to its new owner.

"You're too kind," she said.

"I'm really not," he replied. He took the package with reverence and added softly, "But I'd like to be better."

He gave her a small smile, appearing almost shy. "Thank you for this," he said.

He started to turn away, and Hope spoke impulsively. "Mr. Stein."

He looked back at her.

"Do you mind if I ask..." Hope hesitated then plunged ahead. "Do you mind if I ask where you're taking it? The book, I mean."

"I'm not taking it anywhere. It's taking me." That funny little smile was still on his face. "We're going home."

CHAPTER 6

DECEMBER 2007

Mae

Mae offered more food and coffee to Sharon and Levi, but they declined, and she didn't push it. They were all tired and somewhat discouraged. Sharon had an early shift the following morning, and Levi looked nearly dead on his feet. Mae felt for him. He was probably anticipating a nice bonus when he found that book, and Christmas was right around the corner.

She watched the two sets of taillights disappear into the night, then she closed the door, feeling unexpectedly bereft. She looked for Ruby and found the cat sulking on the sofa, with her back to the room and her ears pointed out to the sides like horns.

Mae laughed and scooped Ruby into her arms. Ruby gave an indignant wail but then quickly relaxed and started purring, pleased to be the center of attention once more. Mae carried her into the kitchen so they could both have a bedtime snack.

"I know," she crooned as they walked. "We ignored you all evening. And you liked Levi, didn't you?"

Ruby squeezed her eyes closed. Mae took the expression as agreement and sighed.

"I liked him too."

The next day was Saturday, always a busy morning at the café. Between greeting customers and taking orders and pouring coffee, Mae filled Donaghy and Trina in on the activities of the night before. She hadn't intended to, but Donaghy hadn't been able to resist telling Trina about the private investigator who had come to see Mae the day before.

"So why does his client want the book?" Trina asked. They were in the kitchen. Trina, a round, pretty, energetic young woman who wore her blond hair in a short, practical style, was waiting to pick up an order.

Mae shrugged as she put freshly sliced bread into the toaster. "As a gift, maybe, or just for a personal collection? I'm not sure. And since I don't have the book, I guess my part in the adventure is over."

"Too bad," Trina lamented. "We could use some excitement in this town."

"You two grew up in Angel River," said Mae. "Do you know anything about this book?"

"I read it in high school," Trina said. "I liked it."

Donaghy turned sausage patties and broke eggs onto the grill to scramble. "I never read that one," he said, "but I read *Lucky Penny*, and it was pretty good."

"Is that another one of Weidler's books?" Mae asked.

The two young people glanced at each other, wearing small smiles. Mae said, "What?"

"It's just always funny to meet someone who doesn't know his work," Trina said. "It's such a thing in this town."

"So you're saying that my outsider status is showing?"

Mae was amused, but also just a little bit hurt. How long would she have to live here before people forgot she was from out of town?

With careless expertise, Donaghy flipped the food onto waiting plates and set them on the pickup counter. Then he rang the order-up bell, even though Trina was only standing two feet away. She rolled her eyes at him, and he grinned.

"Don't worry about it," he said to Mae. "Everyone knows you're a part of this community. But if you want to find out more about Weidler, you should go to the library. There's, like, a whole section dedicated to him."

Trina set the plates on a tray and took them out to the waiting customers. Donaghy turned back to the grill. And Mae murmured, "Go to the library to find out about a writer? Now there's a concept."

ALTHOUGH MAE TOLD HERSELF SHE COULDN'T SPARE THE TIME, as soon as the breakfast crowd started to lighten, she took off her apron, informed Trina she would be right back, and slipped out the front door. The Angel River Library was only a few blocks away, after all, and the day was clear and crisp, winter at its best. It would be a nice a walk, if nothing else. She lifted her face to the sun, feeling the pleasant counter-point of the warmth against the coolness of the air.

Main Street bustled with life. Cars trundled down the street, people moved in and out of shops, carrying packages, chatting on their phones or to live companions. Mae breathed deeply, happy to be alive, pleased to be walking down this sidewalk on this lovely day in this lovely town. There was no place she would rather be. The only thing that would make it better was if her mother were here to share it with her.

At that thought, a cloud moved over her own personal

sunlight, but she mentally blew it away and turned briskly onto the quiet, tree-lined street that was home to the library. In contrast to the activity and noise of Main Street, inside the library all was hushed and calm with that special, magical scent that must be both unique and common to libraries all over the world.

Mae smiled when she saw the familiar face behind the information desk. "Ms. Maud," she said as she crossed the carpeted floor.

The woman behind the counter looked up, and a responding smile of greeting lit her face. But it was quickly chased away by a stark frown and a finger to the lips.

"Keep your voice down," Ms. Maud said. "This is the library."

"Sorry," Mae whispered as she arrived in front of her friend. She and Ms. Maud had met the previous Christmas. It had been a difficult holiday for both of them, but they had helped each other through it. Ms. Maud had been volunteering at the library since the spring, and the position suited her. Today she looked every inch the stern librarian, complete with wire-rimmed spectacles and cameo brooch. Her gray hair had been carefully set in tight curls.

"How are the kittens?" Mae asked.

Ms. Maud's face lit up again, although her features managed to remain self-consciously cranky. "Almost a year old and still too young and rambunctious," she groused drolly. "They'll be better companions when they grow out of adolescence and settle into adulthood."

"I find that's true of most human beings too," Mae responded seriously.

A quiet bark of laughter escaped Ms. Maud's lips, and she covered the slip with a cough. "Are you looking for something in particular today, Mae?"

Ms. Maud possessed limited patience for the company of

anyone, even people she liked, and Mae knew she was being dismissed. She replied, "Actually, I'm hoping to find out a little about that writer, Browning Weidler."

"We have a section devoted to him in the Heritage Room," Ms. Maud said. "I believe we have all of his books and one biography about him, although there's precious little that's actually known about the man."

"Is there anyone on duty back there?"

"Not today, but you can go in. Just don't bring any materials out into the general area of the library. Use the table in the room."

"Okay." Mae smiled. "Good to see you."

Ms. Maud returned the smile with stilted but genuine affection. "You too," she said. "Come back soon."

The Clary County Heritage Room was the section of the library devoted to the research and preservation of the county surrounding Angel River. Its development had been ongoing for several decades and had started with an oral history project to record the memories of some of the area's oldest citizens. There was a fascinating, if somewhat disorganized, collection of materials in the room. Mae knew that the Historical Society had a plan for the organization and development of the collection, but that would have to wait until the local museum was remodeled.

The Heritage Room was toward the back of the building, through the periodicals section, and past nonfiction. The light was on, and the glass door was closed. Mae pushed through. She let the door go, and it shut behind her with what sounded like a soft "shush," as if even the door was reminding her that this was a place for silence.

The room was small but packed to the ceiling with shelves and cabinets. It would be easy to get lost in here, to tiptoe backward through time until one's present seemed dreamlike and unimportant.

Remembering that she had a restaurant to run, Mae forced herself to focus and found the section on Browning Weidler, which turned out to be just two shelves with several copies of the same set of books. *Lucky Penny*, the novel that Donaghy had mentioned, was among them. *The Sound of Silver*, a novelized account of a real silver robbery, was another. Their dust jackets were faded, the formerly shiny paper soft and wooly beneath clear plastic covers.

Tucked in among these was a slim hardback. This one had no dust jacket, and its spine was so deteriorated that it was hard to read the title. Mae pulled it out and carefully opened the cover, smiling a little at the squeak of its cellophane wrapper. There, on the first page, was the title: *The Book of Forgotten Angels*.

Holding her breath, she read the first line. "The hand the holds the pen is not truly in charge of the words. The same could be said for God and mankind. Womankind, of course, is a different story altogether since she holds her own pen with such a ferocious grasp that surely even our Lord Himself must quake to attempt its direction. But further ruminations on that will have to wait for a different time."

Entranced, Mae turned the pages gently, skimming the story of a poor widower, downtrodden and depressed, whose daughter helps him see the work of angels in the people all around them. Wishing she had more time to spend with the book, Mae made a mental note to see if she could order a copy for herself. Then she slipped the volume back on the shelf, and her hand found the biography that Ms. Maud had said would be there.

Walking Shadow: The Dim Outline of a Writer, by Hope Roebeck. Again, Mae turned to the first page, and she read.

"This biography is not all that it should be. It will undoubtedly leave you feeling unsatisfied, certain that there must be more to the story than has been revealed to you. If so, your own emotions will precisely mirror those of everyone who has undertaken the futile task of researching the writer known as Browning Weidler."

From behind Mae, a voice spoke quietly. "That's an early edition of the biography."

Although she recognized the speaker immediately, the sound of his voice made her jump before she turned around.

"Sorry," Levi said. His face was chagrined. He let go of the door, as she had done a few minutes earlier, and it shushed closed once more. "Didn't mean to scare you."

"I didn't hear the door open, that's all." Mae gripped the book in her hands, trying to overlook a stab of felicity at meeting him here, of all places. "And I didn't expect to see you here."

"I didn't expect to see you either." He smiled. "Did you get curious about our Mr. Weidler?"

"It's hard not to be," she confessed. "Plus, I was feeling kind of left out. All my friends are from Angel River, and they grew up with this guy. I'd never heard of him until yesterday."

"That makes sense." He nodded at the book in her hands. "What do you think?"

"I only read the first paragraph, but it sounds interesting. You said this is an early edition of the biography? How many were there?"

Was there the briefest hesitation before he answered? "I'm not entirely sure," he said at last. "At least two that I know of. My copy has a more modern cover. I haven't read it all the way through. I only got it when I started this job."

"Ah. Well, my curiosity has definitely been piqued. I'm going to get a copy of the biography, and *The Book of Forgotten Angels*, too, if I can find it. Do you know if it's still in print?"

"I don't think so, but I've seen late editions online for not too much money. It had its last printing in the seventies, I think. Right around the time the biography was published."

Automatically, Mae turned the biography over and looked at the picture of the author on the back. Hope Roebeck had a pretty, intelligent face. Her smile was somewhat wry, as if she knew she were engaged in a futile endeavor but couldn't quite help herself.

"I wonder if she has a first edition," Mae said suddenly, holding the book up. "The biographer. Or maybe she knows where you can get one for your client."

Another hesitation. "That's a good idea. I'll check it out. But I still haven't quite given up on finding Abel Stein's copy."

"Have you talked to Mr. Forrester, the estate lawyer?"

"Not since I got to town." Levi shook his head. "The office is closed for the weekend. I'm hoping to get in to see him first thing on Monday, but I guess that will depend on how busy his morning is."

"Of course. So in the meantime, you're here doing some research."

"Trying to stay productive," he agreed.

"Well, I should let you get to it. I need to hurry back to the café, anyway." But Mae felt a curious reluctance to leave him. His color was better this morning, as though he might have gotten some good sleep last night, but there was a tightness to his face and a stiffness to his shoulders that spoke of extreme stress.

Impulsively, she asked, "Would you like me to call his office on Monday and set up an appointment? I worked with Mr. Forrester when I bought my house, so maybe…"

"Maybe he'd be more inclined to see you than me," Levi finished for her. His eyes lit with new optimism. "Are you sure you wouldn't mind? I'm guessing Monday mornings at the café can be hectic."

"It doesn't take long to make a phone call," she assured him. "And my staff will cover if I have to pop out. It will be fine."

"I feel like I should tell you not to trouble yourself, but to be honest, I really appreciate the offer, and I think I'll take you up on it."

"Good." Feeling pleased with herself, Mae slid the biography back on the shelf. "And if you get hungry later, come by the café. I'll make sure you get a table."

One corner of his mouth twisted up in a droll smile that reminded her of something. "Really?" he asked. "You have that kind of pull?"

"I know the owner. She's open to bribes."

He laughed slightly. "How can I refuse?"

CHAPTER 7

When Mae got back to the café, the dining room was empty. She found Trina and Donaghy in the kitchen with cups of coffee and half-eaten pie on the counter. Trina was looking over Donaghy's shoulder as he showed her his phone.

"Hard at work, I see," Mae teased.

Trina laughed. "Donaghy just got an iPhone, and he can't stop showing off."

"I didn't hear you complaining," he said.

"I was hypnotized by the hugeness of the screen," she replied smartly. To Mae, Trina added, "The last of the breakfast rush just left, so we're taking a breather."

That made sense. It was rare to catch a break like this, and she didn't begrudge them the rest. Mae stowed her purse and coat in her office then decided to join them. She put on her apron, poured herself a cup of coffee, debated whether to have pie, then decided to skip it. She didn't have the metabolism of a twentysomething anymore.

Donaghy looked at her over his phone. "How was the library? Did you find anything interesting?"

"I found a biography of Browning Weidler, but it was in the Heritage Room, so I couldn't borrow it. Can you help me find a copy online? The author's name is—"

"Hope Roebuck?" Donaghy asked. As soon as she'd mentioned biography, he'd started tapping on his screen.

"That's right," Mae said. "Do you know her work?"

He held up his little device. "My phone does," he said. "I found it online. Should I order it for you?"

"Please," Mae said. "And thanks." After a second, she added, "Do they have *The Book of Forgotten Angels* on there?"

Another tap on the screen. Donaghy said, "The cheapest used copy is eighty-five dollars."

"Wow," Mae said. "I guess I'll pass. If I want to read it, I'll have to log some time in the Heritage Room. Or maybe Levi will let me borrow the first edition when he finds it."

Trina and Donaghy exchanged a surreptitious glance. It was fast, but Mae caught it. "What?" she said.

"You should hear your voice when you say his name," Trina said. She made her tone husky and soft. "*Levi.*"

"I don't sound like that," Mae objected. But she could feel her cheeks getting hot. She turned away, pretending to look for something on the counter, hoping that they wouldn't notice any heightened color on her face.

"Do too," Donaghy said, eyes locked on his phone once more.

"You two are impossible." Mae kept her voice light, but she felt a smidge of annoyance. *Did* she sound like that? She couldn't help but issue a mild rebuke: "You guys are my employees, right? Shouldn't you be too afraid of me to say things like that?"

Out of the corner of her eye, she saw them both shrug. No, apparently they weren't in the least afraid of her.

All right, then. Mae took a breath and turned back to face

them. She cradled her coffee cup in her hands and sipped. "Well, he's coming by later, so just try to be nice, okay?"

Another look passed between the two of them. "*He's* coming by?" Trina asked.

"Yes, *him*. I saw *him* at the library. Poor guy looks like he needs a good meal—or a week of them. I told him he should come over."

"I'll bet you did." Trina grinned.

"Oh, for Pete's sake."

It finally seemed to click with Trina that she was walking a little close to the edge. "I'm just joking," she said quickly. "It's good that he's coming by. And we'll be nice. I promise."

The bell rang out front, saving Mae from having to reply.

"I'll get it," Trina said, still in make-up mode. And she disappeared through the swinging kitchen door before Mae had a chance to reply.

She was back a second later. "It's Mrs. Morrow. She said you were going to make up a box for her?"

"Oh, shoot." The task had completely slipped Mae's mind. She turned to Donaghy. "Can you put together a pastry box? Two dozen assorted of whatever we have. It's for the Ladies Auxiliary meeting or the Historical Society meeting or one of those."

"Sure thing." Donaghy slipped his new pride and joy into his pocket and straightened his apron. He had just grabbed a pastry box when Mae left the kitchen to see her friend.

Violet Morrow was seated at the counter, a silver tea infuser dangling between her fingers. She was one of those women whose age is almost impossible to determine. Her hair, which she wore short, was mostly gray but still had a youthful sprinkling of gold. Her skin was clear and smooth but had started to soften along her jawline. She was as slender as a greyhound, as bright-eyed as a child at Christmas, and as unpredictable as the weather. She was well loved —and slightly feared—by everyone in town.

Trina was setting a mug of hot water down in front of Violet as Mae came through the swinging kitchen doors.

"Rooibos tea," Violet said without preamble when she saw Mae. She dunked the infuser gently into the water, creating a dark billow in the thick white cup. A warm, woody fragrance drifted upward. Looking from Trina to Mae, Violet added, "It's good for the heart and the bones. You should both give it a try. You're young, but you won't be forever."

Mae and Trina exchanged a smile then Mae said to Violet, "I appreciate being grouped into the 'young' category with Trina, but she's at least fifteen years my junior, as you very well know."

Violet's clear gray eyes twinkled. "All you under fifties look the same to me."

Mae wasn't entirely sure that Violet was that far north of fifty herself, but she let it slide. Some arguments weren't worth having.

Violet took another sip of her tea. "How have you been, Mae? Haven't seen you at the shop recently."

Violet owned and operated a health food store called the Purple Carrot, which sold vitamins in every letter of the alphabet as well as organic vegetables that Violet grew herself. They also carried a variety of health foods that could not be found at the Food Grab, their little local grocery story. In addition to running her own business and growing her own food, Violet was also on almost every committee in town, which was why she was picking up pastries this afternoon.

"We've been swamped since Thanksgiving." Mae hoped that would be enough of an excuse for her lack of patronage. What she didn't say was that the last time she had gone into the Purple Carrot, she had walked out with two full bags of health supplements, most of which had gone unused, and she was feeling guilty—both about spending the money, and about not using the products.

"Mm-hmm," Violet said knowingly. "And have you been taking that Brewer's Yeast like I told you to? Best way to get your B vitamins, you know."

"I do take it sometimes," Mae hedged. *Like when I feel like having a mouthful of dirt*, she didn't add. "Although I'm sure not as often as I should."

Violet seemed about to say something else, then must have decided to let it go, much as Mae had let go of the topic of Violet's age. This pick-your-battles mentality was one of the things the women had in common.

Seizing the chance for a change of subject, Mae leaned her elbows on the table. "I saw Ms. Maud at the library today. She looks so happy."

Violet smiled. She was the one who had introduced Mae and Ms. Maud the previous Christmas. "That's good to hear. She deserves some happiness. What did you get from the library? The new Sue Grafton? I have it on hold, so read it quick."

"No, it's not my turn yet. I was there to look at Browning Weidler's books."

"Reading up on our local celebrity, are you?" Violet nodded approvingly. "He was a darn fine writer. Such a pity he wasn't better known."

Donaghy came through the swinging door from the kitchen just as Violet was speaking the last sentence. He carefully set a bulging pastry box down on the counter.

"Well, someone must know Weidler pretty well," he commented. "There's a detective in town looking for one of his first editions."

Mae would have stifled Donaghy's words if she could have, but they were out before she could do anything about it. For some reason, she didn't think that Levi would appreciate his business being casually tossed around, although it was inevitable that people would find out at some point.

Violet set down her mug with a surprised *clink*. Her eyes were round. "A detective? Looking for a first-edition Weidler?" She looked at Mae. "What in heaven is this child talking about?"

"He came to see me yesterday," Mae said reluctantly. Now that the information was out there, she might as well give the honest truth. "The book that his client wants was owned by Abel Stein, and Mr. Morales—the detective—was hoping I might have it."

"And do you?" Violet asked.

Mae shook her head.

Violet flipped open the box of pastries, selected a cinnamon donut, and set it on her napkin before closing the box again. She pushed aside her tea and called to Trina, "Bring me a coffee, hon. I think I'm about to hear a very interesting story, and I need some fortification."

Of course, there wasn't much to tell, but Mae related as much as she knew. She omitted only the amount of money that Levi's client was willing to pay and the fact that Levi was good-looking, intelligent, and seemed a bit desperate to finish this job and get back to wherever he was from. That last bit, Violet would surely find out on her own.

Violet drained her coffee cup thoughtfully. "Well, this is good news for the town, isn't it?"

When the three other people in the room looked confused, she explained, "If someone wants the book that badly, it means that Weidler's name is starting to mean something. And the town could use that kind of legend, you know?"

They nodded. It made sense. Violet said to Mae, "Are you sure you don't have that book?"

"Yes," Mae replied. "I mean, we looked through everything."

"Did you look under the floor in the closet?"

Mae blinked. "What are you talking about?"

Violet chuckled. "Old Abe Stein had a penchant for hidden storage places. I know that he at least had a safe under his closet floor. There are probably more hidey-holes in that house too. You didn't know that?"

"No." This was news to Mae. It was a little bit creepy... but also kind of fun. This was starting to feel like a Nancy Drew novel. What interesting objects might be lurking under her floorboards? Could she have the book, after all?

"Well, you should check everywhere," Violet said. "And ask Mr. Forrester, Abel's lawyer, if you can. He might know something."

"Wouldn't he have had those places cleaned out when the house was sold?" Donaghy asked. He and Trina had been listening raptly, their imaginations obviously piqued by the thought that Mae's house might be full of hidden compartments.

Violet shrugged. "It never hurts to ask."

Mae spoke slowly. "I actually offered to go visit Mr. Forrester on Monday with Le—Mr. Morales." Here, again, she was reluctant to discuss Levi's business, but Violet certainly would find out eventually, anyway.

"Perfect," Violet said. She glanced at her watch and stood up. She made a gesture to Donaghy, which he correctly interpreted as a request to tie up the pastry box so she could carry it more easily. As he got busy with that task, Violet added, "And if you do find the book, you can give it to the museum."

"Wait, what?" Mae thought she must have missed something.

"The Angel River Museum," Violet explained patiently. "It will make a valuable exhibit piece."

Mae was still confused. "But Levi's client—"

"Is not our concern," Violet said flatly. She hefted the pastry box, waving away Trina's offer to help her carry it. Then she turned back to Mae. "That book is part of our heritage. It belongs to the town, not to some anonymous rich person who's never lived here. It's not a curiosity piece, Mae. It's an artifact from Angel River history."

Violet glanced at Trina and Donaghy and added, "Anyone who loves this town would agree, I'm sure."

With that parting thrust, she crossed the room, calling "Tootles," over her shoulder before she pushed through the door.

CHAPTER 8

*L*evi spent several futile hours at the library, reviewing facts that he already knew. When he was done in the Heritage Room, he made use of the library's internet and caught up on his email, before going on to microfiche and making a half-hearted attempt to research Abel Stein yet again.

It was a pointless exercise, of course. Even if he had discovered some hitherto unknown bit of information, it would not have helped him find what he was looking for. He just hated being idle, and he had nothing but time until Mr. Forrester's office opened on Monday.

Finally, restless and frustrated, he zipped up his coat and headed for the exit. As he passed the information desk, the elderly woman behind the counter gave him a hard stare, as though he was the chief suspect in a crime he knew nothing about.

Story of his life.

Levi had a phone call to make, but he wasn't quite ready to face it yet. Feeling the need for both distraction and exercise, he spent some time walking around Angel River. The town, though a little self-consciously picturesque, had a storied charm that couldn't fail to please. The effect was enhanced by a large white house that sat on a distant hill, far enough away to retain an air of mystery but close enough to be a dominant factor in the landscape. There was a story behind that house, he was certain, but he doubted that he would be here long enough to find out what it was. Too bad.

He was surprised and a little disappointed to find that Angel River didn't have a bookstore. He'd wanted to browse a little bit. This case was giving him the itch to read something deep and intense.

As Levi had told Mae on the previous night, he had little use for the classics. The one exception was *A Christmas Carol*, by Charles Dickens. As a child, he'd seen the TV movie with George C. Scott, and had been completely entranced by the story. The idea of recovering one's humanity through the grace of a holiday like Christmas, which was already magical to children, filled him with a sweet, questing kind of peace.

After seeing the movie, he'd tried to read the book but had collapsed under the weight of Dickensian verbiage. In high school, he'd tried again but had been too distracted by girls to make much sense of it. Finally, when he was in college, the timing was right. He'd picked up the book and found himself fully immersed. He had flowed with the language, waltzed with the characterization, and had tiptoed, soft footed in imagination, through the snow-covered settings.

Reading *A Christmas Carol* was one of the most satisfying literary experiences of his life. Levi would have given anything for a distraction like that right now. He should have seen if the library would have given him a temporary card.

Then he remembered the distrustful gaze of the woman behind the counter, and he grinned slightly as he imagined having *that* conversation. Would she have allowed one of the town's precious books to leave the sacred space of the library and be carried off by a total stranger? Someone who, by his own admission, would only be in Angel River for a few more days? Not likely. The woman had looked as if she would guard those books like a dragon guarded gold. Which, as he thought about it, made total sense.

Levi's grin faded and his feet slowed as he caught sight of Mae's café on Main Street. The green awning over the door fluttered in welcome like a waving hand. Through the plate-glass windows, he thought he could see Mae, her brown hair glinting in the light and her smile flashing as she laughed at something a customer said. But maybe it was just his imagination.

She had invited him to come by for a good meal, and he wanted to do just that. He wanted to walk through that front door and see her eyes light up in greeting, smell coffee and cinnamon and all the strengthening scents that imbued the café with life. He *wanted* to do that, but he knew it would be a bad idea. He liked Mae too much, found her too interesting. Her presence was cheerful and comforting, and he was a man badly in need of cheer and comfort. It wouldn't be fair—to either of them—for him to go in there right now.

So he walked on, past the café. And he thought about some things while he avoided thinking about others.

Eventually, the waning daylight told him that he could no longer avoid the inevitable. He returned to his car and drove back to his temporary lodging.

The Harold Smith Motel was a small but sprawling place on the western side of town, just outside of the sign that read, "Welcome to Angel River." It was a brick building, with a central section that was two stories tall and was decorated with white pillars that supported a second-floor balcony. From this grand structure sprang two arms, one story each. They ran perpendicular to the center, then crooked inward at right angles to form a courtyard parking lot. There was a fenced-off pool in the middle of the lot which looked as if it had not seen water in many a year.

Levi assumed that the motel had been built in the early fifties, during the golden era of the family road trip. Although it had obviously been updated sometime in the past five decades, it still had remnants of the days before air conditioning and portable calculators. Under other circumstances, Levi might have enjoyed the unintentionally kitschy touches, like the bottle opener on the wall by the front door, and the illuminated sign on the outside that told the world that the motel had color TVs in every room. Which, on reflection, meant that it had definitely been remodeled after the 1970s. He could imagine coming here in the summer, maybe convincing the owner to fill the pool, and drinking a Coke out of a thick glass bottle as he contemplated times gone by.

But the good old days had only been good to some people, and now, in the bleakness of winter, with everything gray and gloomy, both outside and within himself, the place felt stark and alien.

Levi let himself into his room, and before he even took off his coat or sat down, he pulled out the phone and made the call he'd been dreading.

After one ring, his sister picked up the phone. "Well, it's about time," was all she said.

He took a beat before replying. "How is she?" he asked quietly.

"Who?" Ruth said. "Oh, you mean our mother? She's just great. Nice to know you care."

"Ruth—" he began, but she didn't give him a chance to finish.

"Where *are* you?" Her voice quavered. The fury had run

itself out, and only fear and grief remained. She sounded like a frightened child, and he knew exactly how she felt.

"I told you I had an—"

"Emergency case, I know." Anger flared briefly in her voice again. "I don't understand you, Levi. You leave without warning, drive off to God knows where, and then you don't even call? Mom's in the *hospital*, big brother. She may not have much time left. You're supposed to be here. I'm not supposed to be doing this by myself."

He dropped onto the bed, legs giving way under the weight of his conscience. He lowered his head onto his free hand.

"I'm sorry, Ruthie," he said. "I know I should be there. But this is important. This could help."

"Help who? Mom? She doesn't need your money. She needs your presence."

"And she'll have it." He roused himself. "I'll be back in a few days. I promise. I just have to find something for someone, and then I'll be right home."

"Great," Ruth said bitterly. "I guess we'll see you when we see you."

She hung up, and Levi slowly lowered the phone to his lap. Maybe he should give up on this book and just head back to Wyoming. What was he doing here, anyway? What kind of brother was he? What kind of son?

The thought was so compelling, the guilt so complete, that before he knew what he was doing, he was on his feet and walking to the closet for his suitcase.

The phone rang again. When he saw the number, he answered right away. But before he could utter a word, a voice spoke.

"Levi," his mother said.

He felt the grief wash up like an ocean surge, threatening

to spill over his masculine fortification and flood him with helpless tears. He pulled himself together.

"Hi, Mom," he said, keeping his tone steady and calm. "How are you feeling? I'm just packing up. I'll be home tomorrow night, okay?"

"I called to tell you to stay where you are." She sounded tired, exhausted even. But the undercurrent of steel that had carried her through life was still there.

Levi started to object. "But Ruthie said—"

"Your sister is upset. She's not thinking clearly. The doctors say I'm doing well, all things considered. Yes, I'm going to die, but so are we all." She drew a long, labored breath. "You're on a case?"

"I was," he replied.

She ignored his implication. "And it's important? What you're doing, you're finding something important for someone?"

"It is," he admitted. "I think so, at any rate."

"Well then, son, stay until you finish the job. You're not going to do me any good by sitting around waiting to see if I'll die."

That hurt. "I wasn't going to—"

"I know," his mother said gently. "I was just teasing. But I mean what I say. You should stay where you are and finish what you have to do. I promise to live until you get back. I'm not quite done bossing you around yet, you know."

He laughed through his tears. "If you're sure..."

"I'm sure," she said firmly. "Stay until your job is done. Then come home and see me."

CHAPTER 9

The first thing Mae did upon returning home was to start looking for hidden compartments under the floor. She found none, and ended up feeling like quite an idiot, crawling around and rapping the floorboards with her knuckles. Violet must have been having her on. It seemed like an unnecessary joke—and not very funny. Frankly, Mae wouldn't have credited Vi with the imagination to come up with a gag like that, but it wasn't the first time she'd been surprised by human behavior, and she supposed it wouldn't be the last.

On Monday, she kept her promise to Levi and arrived at Mr. Forrester's office late in the morning. Levi was already there, sitting on the small sofa in the waiting room. He had one ankle propped on the opposite knee, and he must have been flipping through a magazine, because it lay open on his lap.

When she entered the room, he looked up and smiled with relief. He was dressed in khakis and wore a blazer over a white dress shirt. His tie, maroon with navy stripes, brought out the color in his cheeks and made his dark hair glint in the florescent light. Mae's heart did a little tap dance.

"You're here," he said. "I was afraid you wouldn't make it."

"Of course, I'm here," she replied in a don't-be-silly voice. Then, before sitting down next to him, she crossed the room to the reception desk to greet Mr. Forrester's secretary, Jennifer.

"Morning, Mae." Jennifer wore her usual lovely smile. She was a pixie in her mid-thirties with short, neat hair and the patient air of a kindergarten teacher.

"Hey there, Jen." Mae set a cardboard cup and a white paper bag on the desk. "I brought you a little something."

Jennifer's eyes widened with pleasure. "Ooooh," she almost squealed. "Is it the chai tea?"

"And the sugar cookies that you love," Mae replied. "Just a little thank-you for squeezing us in. I know your calendar is always packed."

"You didn't have to do that." Jennifer opened the bag and breathed deeply. "But I'm glad you did, anyway. I'll have to put in at least forty more minutes on my bike for these, but it will be so worth it."

Mae grinned. "What's a few extra calories this time of year?"

"Good point." Jennifer took a slow sip of her tea. "The best," she said and sighed. "You can come by any time, Mae."

They laughed together, and Mae went to have a seat next to Levi. He had watched the exchange between the women with neutral interest.

"I see that you were the right person to help me, in more ways than one," he murmured as Mae sank down next to him.

"She who controls the coffee controls the world," Mae teased in a low voice. "Or, in this case, the tea. But Jennifer is a sweetheart. She would have fit us in, regardless."

Mae hadn't seen Mr. Forrester in ages. When she'd first bought her house, he had overseen the purchase on behalf of Abel Stein's estate. Sometimes he and his wife would come into the café, or she would see him at the Food Grab or the Gas'N'Go. But those occasions were rare, and in fact, she had not actually spoken to him in probably a year.

When Jennifer ushered them into the inner office, Mae found that Mr. Forrester had not changed much in the intervening months. He only looked about sixty-five, although she knew he was a good decade older. And in seeing the collection of photographs on the sideboard of his office, Mae realized that he was one of those men who in fact had looked sixty-five since he was about thirty. He was born to be this age and to have this appearance: grave and gray haired, slightly wizened. His suit was dark gray, and his hair was light gray. That was the only real sense of variation about him.

He stood up when they entered. He gave Levi a polite but cool smile as the men shook hands. For Mae, the smile warmed a half degree. And his hand, when Mae shook it, was quite warm.

They sat down, and Mr. Forrester took charge of the conversation, bringing them straight to the point. "Now then, Mr. Morales, I understand you're still looking for that Weidler book. You had no luck finding it in the boxes in Mae's house?"

"Unfortunately not," Levi replied. "We went through everything, and it wasn't there."

For some reason, this statement made Mr. Forrester frown, as though Levi had insinuated that the boxes of books were worthless. Mae jumped in with, "Mr. Stein had some very interesting volumes, though. I set aside a few for myself, and we repacked everything else."

"Yes, Mr. Stein had good taste in literature," Mr. Forrester replied, somewhat mollified. "He and I spent long nights discussing the merits of Faulkner over Fitzgerald or vice versa, depending on our mood."

Mr. Forrester cracked a dry smile, and Mae laughed politely. "I wish I'd known him," she said. "What was he like?"

"Interesting fellow. A bit eccentric."

"Did you ever talk about the Weidler book?"

"Oh yes," Mr. Forrester said. "He was quite pleased to own it. One of only a half-dozen copies, I believe. It was his prize, to be sure."

"And you have no idea what happened to it?"

"I'm afraid not, my dear. As I told Mr. Morales when we spoke on the phone, when Mr. Stein passed on, I was surprised that the book wasn't on the inventory of his estate. I assume the assessor must have missed it. I wish I had been more diligent at the time, but oh well."

Levi spoke again, tension in his voice. "Doesn't it put you in somewhat of a sticky situation? I mean, you are the custodian of his estate, and it is a very valuable book."

Mr. Forrester gave Levi a cold stare. "For all I know, Mr. Stein gave that book to someone and forgot about it. Old age does make one forgetful, you know. I took every legally obligated step needed to ensure the proper handling of his possessions. The estate has been closed for several years now, and his heirs have never complained."

"Who were his heirs, if you don't mind my asking?" Mae asked quickly, hoping to forestall an argument. "Maybe they might have an idea of where the book is."

Mr. Forrester hesitated then asked, "And why do you want to know about the book, Mr. Morales? You have a client, you told me. What's his interest in Weidler?"

"He's a collector, and he's hoping to give it to someone close to him for Christmas," Levi said. "It was a spur-of-the-moment assignment. I usually don't take this type of case, but in this instance, I felt... compelled by my client's sincere desire for the book."

"Lot of effort for a hundred and fifty pages, if you ask me," Mr. Forrester said stiffly. But then he added, "Although I can certainly relate to dealing with the vagaries of clients. I could tell you some stories."

Levi smiled. "I'm sure you could," he said. "And I appreciate your understanding. I'm sorry if I seemed rude. I would very much like to finish this assignment and get back to my family as soon as possible."

At the word "family," Mae's heart sank just a little. It suddenly occurred to her that just because Sharon hadn't given her any particulars about his marital status didn't mean there was no status to give. And apparently, he had family, someone waiting for him. Maybe even several someones—as in, a wife and kids.

Had Mae even asked Sharon about that? No, of course not. It hadn't seemed important at the time. And that wasn't the moment to be dwelling on such details. Mae tuned back into the conversation.

Mr. Forrester was saying, "Oh, certainly, young man. No hard feelings at all. As I said, I wish I could help. Mr. Stein had his own way of doing things, and my suspicion is that he made a gift of the book and never recorded it. Or possibly he sold it when he did renovations on his house."

"Renovations?" Mae asked, intrigued. "I thought he built that house from the ground up."

"Oh no," Mr. Forrester said. "The cabin was built when he bought it. He added on and did improvements. Central air-conditioning, upgraded electrical, that kind of thing. And carpentry of some kind."

"Like secret hiding places?" Mae smiled in spite of herself. Her knees were still sore from crawling all over her bedroom, but she'd started to see the situation as funny rather than annoying.

Mr. Forrester's eyes twinkled. "It could be." He tapped the side of his nose with his forefinger.

"Did your assessor find anything like that when he inventoried the house?"

"There was a floor safe in the closet, if I remember. But other than that, nothing out of the ordinary."

"Really?" Mae was surprised. She'd expected a simple "no" and had asked the question just to be thorough. Was Mr. Forrester mistaken, or had Mae just missed something?

Before she could voice the thought, Levi asked, "I know it's unusual, but would it be all right if we asked his heirs about the book? I understand he didn't have children, but…"

"No children," Mr. Forrester agreed. "Just some cousins and one close friend. I suppose I could get in touch with them to see if they would be willing to talk to you. Since time is of the essence, Mr. Morales, I'll call them today."

There wasn't much more that Mr. Forrester could do for them. Mae could see Levi searching for more questions to ask, something that might further his search. Finally, resignation descended over his features, and he stood up.

Mae and Mr. Forrester stood too. The three of them said their goodbyes, and Mae and Levi walked back into the reception room. Jennifer was on the phone, but she gave a little wave and smile, which Mae returned.

Mae led the way out to Court Street. On the sidewalk, she paused and studied her companion. His face was grave, his shoulders slumped. He looked like a man on the verge of giving up.

Suddenly, she couldn't take it anymore. "What's really going on with this book?" she blurted.

He blinked at her, as if trying to rouse his thoughts from a million miles away. "What?"

Mae crossed her arms over her chest. "I've been telling myself that it's none of my business, but you did knock on my door at five o'clock in the morning, and you did spend four hours going through boxes in my house. You also offered me a nice sum of money to help you find what you're looking for. So I guess maybe it *is* my business, and I want to know. What is really going on here?"

For a moment, it seemed as though Levi might not answer. He spent several minutes inspecting the bark of one of the large maple trees that were planted along the sidewalk on Court Street. The trees were old, their roots pushing through the brick of the sidewalk in places. Mae had a fleeting thought that the trees, quiet in their leafless torpor, were nonetheless listening, holding their breath and waiting for Levi to say something.

Finally, he obliged. "My mother's sick." He rubbed the back of his neck wearily. "She's in the hospital. My sister is bearing the full brunt of the situation, and I need to get back for both of them."

"Your mother and your sister," Mae repeated. "That's the family you were telling Mr. Forrester about?"

Levi nodded. "For some reason, I thought this would be an easy job, you know? Very few people are interested in Weidler. The latest catalog of the Antiquarian Booksellers of America listed six known copies of *Forgotten Angels*, and one of them is supposed to be here in this town. I arrogantly assumed that you would have it or that someone would know what happened to it. But every road I've traveled has turned into a dead end. And the longer it takes to find the book, the harder it is for me to concentrate. I'm beginning to realize that I might not be able to find it before Christmas, and I can't stay away from home much longer."

There was a long moment of silence during which Levi caught his breath, and Mae considered how best to reply.

At last, she said simply, "I'm so sorry about your mother."

He swallowed. "Thank you."

"May I ask—"

"Breast cancer," he replied brusquely. "She's been fighting it for years."

"That's how I lost my mom," Mae murmured. Her old grief, still deep and raw after six years, surged out of nowhere: a ravening beast, intent on devouring her peace of mind. She patted it down, put it away, and focused on the man in front of her.

He was watching her closely, she realized. Silence grew between them again, but this time it was watchful and heavy with something that Mae had not felt in some time. It was the silence of two people who are suddenly aware that a mere acquaintanceship might become something more.

She was about to speak when he said, "Would you like to have dinner with me?"

The invitation was so unexpected that Mae laughed. "I was just about to suggest you come back to the café with me and have a bite to eat."

He smiled faintly. "I appreciate the offer, but that's not what I'm thinking. I'm thinking I'd like to sit at a table with you in a place where someone brings you food instead of vice versa. I'd like to see you eat a meal without looking around to check on everyone in the dining room. And I'd like to have a conversation with you that isn't centered on that bloody book. What do you say?"

Mae felt herself blush. Was this a date? Was she being asked out on a date? Did it matter? No, it didn't. She lifted her chin, and with a smile in her heart, she said, "Sure. That sounds nice."

CHAPTER 10

$\mathcal{T}$he Golden Dragon, Angel River's only Chinese restaurant, was located at the end of a mini mall on the west end of town, not far from Levi's motel. He wanted to treat Mae to something that was as far from home cooking as he could, and she assured him that the food was good, so they settled on it as the place for dinner.

Levi felt strangely nervous as he walked the half mile along Route 2347. He had decided to leave his car at the motel, hoping to work off a little of his anxiety by stretching his legs. The nerves and anxiousness might have been due to the urgency he felt to finish this job and get home. Or it might have been because he didn't want to finish the job and leave Angel River. Or maybe it was just because he was about to go on his first date in… well, more months than he wanted to count.

As he reached the mall and stepped up onto the curb, he caught sight of Mae's Volvo, which was just pulling into a parking space near the restaurant. Suddenly, an entirely new kind of nervousness seized him. Did *Mae* realize that this was a date? Had he made it clear when he had asked her out that he was, well, asking her out?

"For Pete's sake, man, pull yourself together," he muttered.

He watched Mae emerge from her car. Her hair had been brushed to a high gloss, and her graceful shoulders were set off by the natty fit of her green wool coat. At the sight of her, Levi's worry fled, and a simple determination descended.

If Mae didn't realize this was a date yet, he would make sure she knew it as soon as possible.

They exchanged greetings, and he held the door for her as they went inside. The restaurant was dim and cozy, fragrant with garlic and hot oil. Christmas music played softly in the background. After they hung their coats in a little alcove off the foyer, the hostess showed them to a booth. She waited until they were seated then handed them menus and told them the waitress would be right over.

As soon as she was gone, Levi gathered his courage, looked Mae straight in the eyes and said, "By the way, this is a date."

She halted in the middle of putting her napkin in her lap. After the briefest of pauses, she finished guiding the linen downward. She looked back up at him, and her cheeks flushed slightly, giving him a little thrill.

When she spoke, her voice was casual. "All right, then," she said.

"I just wanted to make it clear," he went on, feeling the need to explain. "Because a man my age can't afford to assume in these situations."

That made her laugh. "*People our age* certainly can't," she agreed drily.

The waitress appeared at that moment. She was a pleas-ant-looking young woman with dark hair pulled smoothly off her forehead, and she had a red apron wrapped around her waist. She was carrying two stemmed glasses of ice water, which she deposited on to the table with a gentle *clink*.

They ordered drinks—red wine for Mae, beer for Levi—and the waitress promised she would be right back.

When she was gone, Mae leaned forward slightly and smiled. She said, "I appreciate the clarity about this being a date. And I'm glad it is."

Something in his chest loosened at her words.

She went on, "And just so we continue to be on the same page, let me ask a question. What does 'being on a date' entail, exactly? It's been a while for me, to be honest."

"That makes two of us for the 'been a while' part, then. So, let's see." Levi picked up his water and sipped thoughtfully. "Okay, well, first of all, I invited you, so I'm paying for dinner."

For a moment it appeared that she might argue with that, but then she said, "Fine with me."

Their drinks arrived, and the waitress told them to take their time with the menu. When she was gone, Levi picked up again right where he'd left off.

"I don't expect a kiss good night, of course, but I may want to go for a walk and hold your hand later."

"Also fine," Mae agreed, her eyes cast demurely downward.

He finished, "We can share our life stories, but any discussion of exes should be kept to a minimum."

"Extremely fine," Mae said fervently. "Is that it?"

"On my end, yes," Levi said. "What about you?"

Mae considered. "No cell phones unless it's an emergency."

"Agreed." Although as Levi said the words, he remembered that Abe Stein's attorney had said he might call.

"Of course, Mr. Forrester is an exception," Mae said, reading his mind.

He smiled gratefully. "Sounds good. Anything else?"

"Just one thing." Mae picked her menu back up and studied it carefully. "That kiss good night is at my discretion."

Levi followed her example and lifted his menu. "I wouldn't have it any other way," he said.

OVER EGG ROLLS AND HOT-AND-SOUR SOUP, LEVI LEARNED that Mae had only been living in Angel River for six years. Before that, she had lived in Chicago.

"That's a big move," Levi said.

"Yes, it was" Mae replied. She paused, then added, "My mother passed away, and I decided I needed a change of scenery. And not to violate tonight's rule about exes, but my marriage ended around the same time."

"I'm sorry, on both accounts."

"I asked him to come with me. I thought it could be a fresh start for us. But he wasn't interested. Not in moving, or in staying married." A faint mist gathered in her eyes. She blinked it away and met Levi's gaze. Her color rose slightly as she smiled. "But I guess things turn out the way they're supposed to."

His skin tingled at her smile, at what he wanted the expression to mean. "What was it like for you to move here, to start over?"

"Incredibly difficult—and incredibly worth it," she answered promptly. "I haven't loved every minute of it, but I've learned a lot about myself." Her eyes turned wistful. "And I love this town."

"Are you ever lonely?"

The question was out of his mouth before he had a chance to think about it. Immediately, he added, "I'm sorry. That was unbelievably presumptuous."

"It's okay," Mae said with hurried politeness. "Natural thing to wonder about a single woman in her forties."

"It's not that." He had really put his foot in it. The only thing that might save him now was the truth. So that was what he gave her. And once the words started coming, it was impossible to stop them. "It's that *I'm* lonely. I've been lonely for a long time, and I didn't realize it until just now, and the question just popped out of my mouth, and wow, this is incredibly embarrassing. Excuse me while I crawl under the table."

"Oh sure, because that's the way to make this situation less awkward." Mae chuckled. She reached out and touched his hand.

"I do get lonely sometimes," Mae said reassuringly. "And there's nothing embarrassing about that."

Her touch was a casual gesture, light and friendly and nothing more. But suddenly the room seemed brighter, the colors around him richer and more beautiful. Levi felt his world open with that touch, felt like he could dive into the ocean of her eyes and swim there forever.

Oh, Lord help him, he was falling for this woman. Falling hard. It had snuck up on him so quickly that he hadn't even realized what was happening.

But it *couldn't* happen. Not now, and maybe not ever. Levi knew that as surely as he knew anything. He had to finish this job and get home to see his mother. And then he had to work out how to make some changes in his life.

If there were women like Mae in the world, Levi wanted to get his act together so that he might one day deserve to be with one.

THEIR MAIN COURSE ARRIVED, AND THE TALK TURNED TO FOOD and travel and the restaurant business. Levi had a few amusing anecdotes up his sleeve having to do with investigation, and he shared them liberally, enjoying the way Mae's eyes crinkled when she laughed.

Eventually, she asked, "So do you like this rare book investigation? The mystery of it all?"

He toyed with his chopsticks, trying to figure out how best to answer. "Rare books are a world unto themselves," he said finally. "I've barely scratched the surface. There is a lot of romance wrapped up in old books, and as you said, there's a lot of mystery too. People get very obsessed."

"That's because we don't just read books, we fall in love with them," Mae replied. "Finding a good book is like finding new love. You walk around in the haze of this new universe you've discovered. You want to tell everyone about it, but you also want to keep it to yourself because it's so fascinating and perfect that you're not sure you're quite ready to share it. And once you do start talking about it, you can't stop. People roll their eyes and try to change the subject. But you don't care because you know that what you've found is real and rare. It's something no one can take away from you."

The words had flowed out of Mae like fine wine: dark and silky, smooth and deep. All at once she seemed to become aware of what she was saying. Embarrassment and consternation flooded her features.

She gave a half laugh. "And that's why I never have more than two glasses of wine when I go out. I tend to wax poetic when I drink." She cleared her throat and reached for her glass of water. "Sorry about that," she said when she'd had a sip.

"Why?" Levi asked, perplexed. "Please, keep waxing. It's beautiful, what you were saying. And very true."

Silence fell between them, thick with possibilities. A delicate shift came into the air, and a wordless conversation seemed to take place.

I like you, Mae. A lot.
I like you too.
I wish...
I wish too.
But we can't.
I know.
For a lot of reasons.
I know. It's okay.

It wasn't really okay. Not with him, at any rate. But what choice did he have?

CHAPTER 11

*W*as she lonely?

Mae had scoffed internally at the question when Levi asked it, had avoided looking too deeply for her answer, giving him a reply that was philosophically accurate but maybe not precisely true. She'd thought the matter was closed, but it must have been revolving in her mind throughout dinner and on her way home. As she crossed her threshold, locking the door behind her with a decided snap, the question came back abruptly.

Was she lonely?

She hung up her coat and went in search of Ruby. Usually, the cat met her at the door, demanding food and attention and other worshipful ministrations. But occasionally, Mae found her asleep, curled up on the sofa and oblivious to the world. This had become more common during the past year. Mae knew it was a sign that her beloved pet was starting to get old.

Now, as Mae found Ruby curled up and snoring lightly, she extended a hand, stroked the silky fur, and tried not to think about the day when Ruby wouldn't wake up, and Mae would have to come home to an empty house.

Yes, she finally admitted to herself. Yes, she was lonely.

In her back pocket, her phone chirped. Mae pulled it out and sat down on the sofa. Levi had sent her a text message.

Just talked to Mr. Forrester. Have an appointment to see one of the heirs tomorrow.

Mae glanced at her watch. It was after nine. Impressive that Mr. Forrester would still be working so late at his age.

Impulsively, she hit the button to call Levi. Then she wondered what she was doing, why she hadn't just texted back and been done with it. Desperate, much?

She winced internally and was about to disconnect the call when two things happened at once. One was that Levi answered the phone, his rich voice coming across the cold night and warming her from the inside as he said, "Hello?"

And the other thing that happened was that Ruby woke suddenly, giving her customary yowl of combined annoyance and greeting.

Levi must have heard the cat through the phone, because he immediately said, "Ruby, why are you calling me at this hour?"

Mae smiled and sandwiched the phone against her shoulder as she lifted Ruby into her lap. "Actually, this is Mae," she said. "Hope you're not too disappointed."

"Never," he replied stoutly. "Did you get my text?"

Ruby stretched out and allowed herself to be petted.

"Yep," Mae said. "I was impressed that Mr. Forrester is still at the office at this time of night."

"Me too," Levi said. "Impressed and a little intimidated, to be honest."

"So you have an appointment to see one of Mr. Stein's cousins tomorrow?"

"It's not one of the cousins." There was a pause, probably so he could consult his notes. "It's someone named Wendell Beaufort. Apparently, he and Mr. Stein were childhood friends."

"I know that name." Mae was startled. "He's kind of a recluse. Lives outside of town." Before she could think better of it, she asked, "Do you want me to come with you?"

There was a small silence, and Mae was sure she had overstepped.

"Of course not," she said immediately. "You don't need me. You know what you're doing."

"I can assure you that I hardly ever know what I'm doing," he joked. "And as for needing you…"

Another silence, this one stretching until Mae felt a warm flush enveloping her.

"I don't know how to finish that sentence and still keep this conversation on an appropriately casual level," Levi finally said.

"Who says it has to be appropriate?" Mae asked, feeling daring. "Or casual, for that matter?"

When he didn't reply, she knew she had surprised him. Well, that was okay. She had surprised herself too.

Instead of answering her directly, Levi said, "I had a good time tonight, Mae."

"I had a good time too." She knew where this was going. Hadn't there been that moment at dinner when an unspoken conversation had seemed to pass between them? Maybe that had been her imagination, but regardless, their situation was fixed. He was leaving in a few days, and it was uncertain when or if he would be back this way. Neither of them was looking for a casual fling. And that was their situation, in all its complex simplicity.

Before he could say anything, before he could give voice to all the things that shouldn't have to be said, Mae decided to save them both any further embarrassment. Or frustration, for that matter.

"And actually," she said lightly, as if this were a careless continuation of a previous conversation, "I just realized I'm kind of beat. That's what a heavy meal does to you, right?"

"Very true." She could hear the relief in his voice, the unspoken gratitude that she had made the situation marginally less awkward. "And I'm guessing you have an early day tomorrow?"

She did, at that. "Four a.m.," she said, glancing at the mantle clock.

"Ugh, that's early, all right," Levi replied genially. "I guess I should let you off the phone."

"Unfortunately. So..." Mae took a beat, trying to gauge their respective moods. Was this entirely false friendliness, or had they really managed to dispel a potential conversation that neither of them was ready for?

"I appreciate everything you've done for me while I've been here," Levi said suddenly. "I'm not sure I've adequately thanked you. I mean, I know that there is money involved, so it's not entirely altruistic—and I can't blame you one bit for that—but this feels above and beyond. So, thanks. Truly."

Mae exhaled slowly. Okay, it was real friendliness. That part was good. And Levi had just expertly reestablished their relationship as one of congenial business. That part was good too.

So why did it sting, just a little?

Mae said what had to be said. "You're more than welcome. This has been... a fun distraction for me."

"Good," Levi said after a moment. "Is it okay if I swing by the café tomorrow after I see Mr. Beaufort?"

"Of course," Mae replied politely. "There will be a cup of coffee with your name on it."

"That sounds great." Neither of them spoke for a moment. "Are we okay?"

"Of course," Mae said again, her voice bright with determined cheer. "Have a safe drive tomorrow, and I'll see you at the café afterward."

"Great." Both of them seemed to be repeating themselves. Wasn't that about the time when a conversation was officially over?

"Good night, Levi," Mae said softly.

"Good night, Mae," he answered. "Sweet dreams."

CHAPTER 12

ABEL STEIN, 1998

*A*be had learned to trust the whispers. They didn't happen all the time, but that just made them seem more vital, more significant. When the whispering came, he listened.

The first time he'd heard them was when he met Lily Morrow on the playground after school. The fading daylight caught the gold in her hair, her laughter danced on the wind, and suddenly his mind was full of whispers.

They filled the air around him, tumbling voices breathing words he couldn't quite catch. Everything about her whispered to him: the freckles on her nose, the perfect ovals of her fingernails. She'd plucked a buttercup and held it under his chin to see if he liked butter. And the blossom, trembling between her fingers, had also whispered.

They'd just started third grade, and he'd been too young, of course, to really know what love was, too young to feel that heady rush of emotion. And yet, he *had* known, and he *had* felt it. Lily. As beautiful as a flower, as light as a feather. A fairy of a girl, spinning in the sunlight.

Lily.

It was inevitable that she would fall in love with someone else. Abel had never really hoped for reciprocal feelings. He'd merely worshiped her from afar, and that had been enough. The thing he found hard to accept was that the boy for whom Lily had fallen had been his best friend, Wendell. It had made high school unbearable, but he loved Lily too much to be anything other than friends with the two of them.

After graduation, Lily had run away to San Francisco, and Wendell had chased after her. Abe had sought his own escape, joined the army and gone to Vietnam, along with a dozen other young men from town. In their wildest nightmares, they could never have imagined what lay in store for them halfway around the world: the terror and the violence and the rampant, reckless death.

The whispers had saved Abe on more than one occasion. He could barely believe it himself, and he would never dare to say it out loud to any living soul. But how many times had he made a choice to move right or left because the whispers had come from one direction or another? Once Abe had clapped his buddy Malcolm on the shoulder and had heard… no, not whispers, but the lack of them. A stony-cold silence that allowed no echo, no reverberation of hope. Malcolm had died not three hours later, cut down mid laugh by a sniper's bullet.

When Abe's time as a soldier was done, he had been shipped back to his home country. Wrecked and ragged but still breathing, it had taken him awhile to realize that he was still alive. And when he was capable of coherent thought, capable of recognizing that he was now expected to continue some semblance of normal life, some of his first thoughts had been of Wendell Beaufort, the sturdy soul who had been his boyhood companion.

He remembered the early days of their childhood, days of bare feet and sun-hot sidewalks and pooling their pennies to buy Eskimo Pies down at the Food Grab. The fact that their easy friendship had dissolved under the radioactivity of their mutual love for Lily no longer seemed important. If he were to go in search of anyone, it would be Wendell.

But Abe could not go back to his hometown. His feet would not carry him there. His body rebelled at the idea of walking those streets or breathing that air. He would not recognize himself there. Too much time had passed, too much blood had been spilled. If he caught sight of himself in a shop window, the strangeness of his own reflection might drive him mad.

And so he got a job as a stock boy at a department store in the city. And one day, on a bus, he picked up an old paperback that someone had left behind. Jack London's *To Build a Fire and Other Stories.*

"Anthology," he thought, calling up the word suddenly from a long-ago English class.

Abe had never been a reader, never found anything particularly appealing about books. But he opened the cover and fell into the story, and after that he never wanted to be anywhere else except inside a book.

It was years later—decades, actually—that the whispers had brought him to *The Book of Forgotten Angels.* By that time, he was well-off but misanthropic. He hoarded his wealth and reveled in his solitary, joyless life. He wanted for nothing. He needed no one. That was the way he liked it.

But when a young-old woman named Hope opened the hundred-year-old cover, it was as if not just the pages of the book had opened, but the pages of his very existence. Suddenly, he had seen inside himself in a new and extraordinary way.

And so, he had gone home at last. When he returned to

town, he wasted no time but went in search of Wendell. He found his old friend at the bottom of a bottle, alone in a deep, dark place.

CHAPTER 13

DECEMBER 2007

Levi

Following the directions that Mr. Forrester had given him, Levi bumped along a wooded country lane, looking for a mailbox that had been painted with an orange flower. When he saw it, he put on his turn signal and steered his car into a driveway that was barely more than a clear place between the trees.

The ground was carpeted with fallen leaves, and the bare branches formed a thick lattice that nearly blotted out the winter-blue sky. Then, all of a sudden, the trees parted, and Levi found himself in a large clearing where two houses sat as if they'd sprung right out of a fairy tale.

Straight ahead of him was a small Victorian masterpiece. It stood on a graceful rise of land, proud but obviously empty, with windows shuttered and front path overgrown. To Levi's left was a Craftsman cottage, downhill from the Victorian, closer to the earth and infinitely less ornamental. And yet the cottage had its own charm, not the least of which was the fact that Levi would never have expected to find any house back here, tucked away in the woods.

He pulled to a stop, unsure what to do next. After a few seconds of staring at the Craftsman, he realized that a man was sitting in a rocker on the front porch. The man's eyes were closed and his head was back. For a moment, Levi was afraid that the man was dead.

Levi turned off the car and stepped out. At the gentle chunk-chunk of the car door closing, the man on the porch twitched, and Levi sighed with relief. Not dead. Just sleeping.

Or passed out, Levi realized as he moved up the short front walk. Although it was just after ten in the morning, the man had a glass in his hand, and a half-empty bottle of Plymouth Royal whiskey at his feet. He also had a shotgun leaning up against the wall of the house within an arm's easy reach.

At the sight of the weapon, Levi stopped walking and decided that a remote greeting was advisable. He pitched his voice so it was loud enough to carry, but hopefully not so loud that it would startle the sleeper into a shooting kind of wakefulness.

"Mr. Beaufort?" he called. No response. He paused and tried again. "Mr. Beaufort?"

The man on the porch stirred slightly. His eyelids fluttered open then closed again immediately, as if the daylight was just too much.

Encouraged, Levi went on. "I'm Levi Morales. Mr. Forrester said I could come see you. It's about Abel Stein."

The man's eyes opened, wider this time. He lifted his head with effort and squinted down at Levi. He must have understood Levi's words, because he waved his hand in an unexpectedly elegant gesture. "Come on up if you're coming," he croaked.

As Levi closed the distance to the porch and mounted the

shallow front steps, Wendell Beaufort closed his fist around his glass and lifted it to his lips. When he lowered it again, he looked slightly more present. "Take a seat," he said.

There was only one chair on the porch, so Levi settled on the top step with his back against the banister, body angled so he could look up at Wendell.

Wendell used his boot to nudge the whiskey in Levi's direction. "Have a sip, if you're so inclined." A brief twinkle appeared in his eye. "I may be a drunk, but never let it be said I'm a bad host."

Levi couldn't help but smile. Wendell was a charmer. Levi just hoped that the man would also be a good source of information.

Giving Wendell a little time to wake up, Levi gazed around at the clearing. From where he sat, he could see the gingerbread on the Victorian house next door. "This is an amazing place," he said. "A little secret spot."

Wendell refilled his glass with a shaking hand and took a deep drink. He sighed as he rested the glass on his knee once more.

"Built in 1941, these were," Wendell said. "Man named Kittlewatt built them for his daughters, who were supposed to be married on the same day in the summer of 1942. Then Pearl Harbor happened, and his would-be sons-in-law went off to war and died. The girls stayed at home with their dad after that, and these houses went empty for years."

"How sad," Levi said, startled by the slew of words that had come out of a man who barely appeared conscious.

Wendell nodded his agreement. "Folks in town have always called these houses The Twin Sisters, on account of the fact that Kittlewatt's daughters were twins and still as unlike each other as these two buildings are. There's a lake, too, back there." He gestured over his shoulder with his glass. "Man-made, of course, and tiny, but it's there. Kittlewatt called it Back of the Moon because it's shaped like a crescent moon."

This second spiel appeared to tire Wendell considerably. He sagged in his chair and lifted his glass, but this time he only sipped.

"Mr. Beaufort," Levi said gently. "Can I get you a glass of water? Or maybe a cup of coffee?"

"Don't drink coffee," Wendell said with that twinkle in his eye again. "It's a bad habit. You're here about Abe, then?"

Relieved he didn't have to be the one to bring up Wendell's departed friend, Levi nodded. "I'm looking for something that used to belong to him."

"That angel book?" Wendell asked promptly.

Levi stared, excitement starting to rise. "Yes," he said. "Do you have it?"

Wendell shook his head, dashing Levi's hopes. "Don't know what became of it, although it was Abe's pride and joy. It was the reason he came back, or so he said."

"Came back?"

"To Angel River," Wendell explained. Observing Levi's mystified expression, he said, "Abe and me, we were friends when we were kids. Kind of went our separate ways after high school. He went off to war, and nobody heard from him for thirty-some years. I went to San Francisco, chasing a girl like a dang fool."

"I'm sorry." Levi didn't know what else to say.

"So am I," Wendell replied drily. "Life is a sad affair, isn't it? By the time you know what you want, by the time you're brave enough and smart enough to go after it, it's gone."

He heaved a deep sigh. "Abe came back to town after he found the angel book up in Boston. He told me that reading that story made him want to be a better man. I never understood it, but I was glad that he came home so we could make up and be friends again. I'll admit I was in bad shape when he found me. He helped me break out of the bottle, stood by me while I cleaned myself up, and left me everything he had when he died. He was a good friend. Since he's been gone, the drink has overtaken me again. But I had a few good years, and that's something."

The words *I'm sorry* hovered again on Levi's lips, but he didn't speak them. They would have been trite and ineffectual in the wake of such a story.

Finally Levi said, "It certainly was generous of him to leave you everything." Something occurred to him. "But wait, aren't there cousins or something?"

"Second cousins." Wendell spat over the railing of the porch, indicating what he thought of them. "They didn't want nothing to do with an old man while he was alive and poor. Once he was dead and rich, suddenly they considered themselves family."

"They didn't know that Abe had money?" Levi heard how the question sounded and hastened to add, "Not that that's an excuse for ignoring him."

"Abe wore old shoes, drove an old car. He counted every penny he spent, and everyone in town knew it. Nothing about him screamed millionaire." Wendell grinned. "Except his bank statement, of course. I guess that old Forrester was the only one who knew Abe had made good. I had no idea he was loaded, myself, until after he passed. Abe willed everything to me, but of course the cousins came shuffling forward with their hands held out. They challenged the will. Mr. Forrester wanted to fight them, but I told him to settle. I don't need much, and I knew Abe wouldn't want his house and things to sit around waiting for a judge's order. Especially not his books. He loved them like they were his real children."

"Like that Browning Weidler book?" Levi asked softly.

"That was his favorite of them all," Wendell confirmed.

His voice dropped an octave. "I'm surprised he didn't make some special provision for it in his final disposition, but between you and me, old Abe's screws were getting a little loose toward the end. He told me once that the book had whispered to him from across the room, and that was the reason he bought it. And I've heard that he had Carl make some crazy hiding places in his house, although that's just rumor."

Levi's heart sank. If Abe Stein's mental faculties had been failing, the book might be anywhere. Or nowhere.

He looked up to find Wendell's gaze resting on him sympathetically. The man's eyes were large and brown, and for a moment, they were also beautifully clear and frank.

"I'm sorry I can't be more help," Wendell said. "For some reason, I think Abe would have liked you."

Something seemed to occur to him. "The one thing I can offer you, if you think it will be of any assistance, is a copy of the estate inventory. It has every blessed thing that was in that house, near as I can tell."

Since Mr. Forrester had already assured him that *Forgotten Angels* wasn't on the inventory, Levi doubted that the list would help him at this point. But he thought it would be rude to turn down the offer.

"I would certainly appreciate it." He glanced toward the rusty screen door. "Is it inside? Do you want me to get it?"

But Wendell had already heaved himself to his feet. "Better not," he replied. "It can be tricky for outsiders to find things in my house. I have a system."

He opened the front door just enough to squeeze inside. Levi wasn't able to get much of a look at the interior, but he did catch a glimpse of stacks and stacks of boxes and papers, crammed in nearly to the ceiling.

System, Levi thought sadly.

He half expected Wendell to disappear inside and not

come back out; lost, perhaps, inside the maze of his own hoarding. But the man reappeared a few minutes later, clutching a grimy file folder in his hand.

He closed the door behind him, in a motion that had an air of tidiness about it, as though Wendell wanted to convey a perfect and cheerful control over his possessions. Levi let him maintain the façade and stood to gratefully accept what was being held out to him.

"That's all the paperwork from the estate," he said. "Keep it. I have copies."

Levi had no doubt that was the case.

He turned to make his way down the stairs then stopped and looked back. "Is there anything I can do for you, Mr. Beaufort? Are you going to be okay?"

Wendell had settled into his rocker once again and was reaching for his glass. He leaned back with a smile on his face.

"Of course, I am, son," he said genially. "We're all okay in the end. Don't you know that?"

CHAPTER 14

At the same time that Levi was winding up his visit to Wendell Beaufort, Mae was pleasantly surprised to see Kate Doyle come into the café. Kate's auburn hair had grown long since she had moved to town, and she was wearing it swept up in a messy bun, casual but elegant. Her small frame was encased in a crew neck sweater and warm leggings. She had an oversized cable-knit scarf around her shoulders. Her pregnant belly protruded sweetly.

"Aren't you cold?" Mae asked, by way of greeting. "I'm pretty sure we've passed the sweater-and-scarf part of the year and are well into full-on coat weather."

Mae was teasing, and Kate obviously knew it. She patted her stomach. "Built-in furnace, right here," she said. "I've come close to turning on the air conditioner at home once or twice in the past few days."

She settled onto a counter stool, and Mae came closer. "What can I get you?"

Kate said. "I don't suppose you have any decaffeinated iced tea, do you?"

"We could make some up, if you have a few minutes," Mae offered. "Want it sweetened?"

"You're a godsend," Kate murmured. "Unsweetened will be great, thanks. I plan to eat my body weight in pastry, so that will fulfill my sugar quotient for the day."

Mae stuck her head into the kitchen and told Donaghy to whip up a pitcher of decaf iced tea, unsweetened.

Predictably, Donaghy asked, "How do I whip tea?" Mae ignored him and returned to the dining room.

Kate asked for a pumpkin muffin to go with her tea. "I've been dreaming about them ever since you brought them to the station the other day," she confessed. "Where did you get the recipe?"

"It was my mother's," Mae said. "Most of the pastries here are based on recipes that she taught me."

Suddenly, Mae missed her mother so much she could barely stand up. She leaned against the counter, trying to look casual. But her distress wasn't lost on Kate.

"What's wrong?" Kate reached out, as if to take Mae's hand, but stopped a few inches away. "Are you feeling okay?"

Embarrassed to have been caught out in such a direct way, Mae started to make an excuse. But then she wondered: why was she always doing that? Why should she make an effort to appear perfectly fine when she was feeling tired and sad and lonely?

So she lifted her chin and told the truth. "The season is getting to me," she said frankly. "I miss my parents, and sometimes I even miss my ex. And recently, I've been wondering if I'm on the right track with my life."

"I'm sorry." Kate moved the final bit of distance, and covered Mae's hand with her own. "I know a thing or two about being lonely in a crowd, feeling out of place in your own life."

Mae looked at her doubtfully, and Kate gave a small laugh. "I'm in a good place now—a wonderful place, really. But there are more than a few lost years in my past, believe me."

In the kitchen, Donaghy rang the pick-up bell, which meant that the iced tea was ready. Mae gave Kate's hand a grateful squeeze then released it so she could go back and retrieve the pitcher.

When she brought it back out, she found that Kate had reached behind the counter and removed two glasses. "One for each of us," Kate said. "Is that okay?"

"It's perfect." Mae set the pitcher on the counter. From the pastry case, she pulled out two pumpkin muffins and put them onto small plates.

Kate patted the stool next to her. "Sit a minute."

The dining room was mostly empty. The lunch rush would be starting soon, but for now the only customers in the café were a few regulars who liked to sit for hours and read the paper or work on their laptops. On the whole, Mae preferred customers who ate, paid, and left to make room for more customers who would eat and pay. But right now, when all she wanted to do was sit and talk, she was grateful for what Trina and Donaghy called the "low-maintenance lurkers."

She settled onto the stool that Kate had indicated and sipped her tea while Kate tucked into her muffin. Kate made a blissful face as she took that first bite. "So perfect," she sighed around her mouthful of food. She fluttered her eyelashes at Mae. "Will you marry me?"

Mae almost did a spit take. "I'm flattered," she said, "but I play for the other team."

"Me too." Kate gave a mock pout. "Too bad. We'd be so perfect for each other."

Mae took a taste of her own muffin. Kate was right—it was amazing. And she could acknowledge that without feeling arrogant, since she hadn't actually done the baking herself. She was merely the architect of deliciousness, not the builder.

"So." Kate took a sip of tea. "If you're missing your ex, it must be a pretty rough time."

Mae laughed. "Oh, it's not that bad. And I don't always miss him, just sometimes. I was hoping he would move here with me, but small-town life had no fascination for him. And truthfully, our lives together were over long before we split up. Inertia, you know? We weren't happy, but we didn't know how to get out of it, and I'm not even sure we realized we had been unhappy together until we split up."

"Facing up to dissatisfaction with your own life can be tough," Kate said with feeling. "And making a big change, like moving someplace where nobody knows you? Phew. I give you a lot of credit for doing that."

"Thanks." Mae had forgotten how great it could be to just talk to someone, especially another woman. Female companionship had been sorely missing in her life the past few years. Then again, she reflected, so had male companionship, although for very different reasons.

"How did you end up in Angel River, anyway?" Kate asked. "You came from Chicago, right?"

"That's right," Mae said. "I was looking for someplace different, and I just started taking long car trips, looking at restaurants that were for sale, getting farther and farther away from home. Eventually I wound up here, and I knew—I just *knew*—that I wanted to stay. The café called to me, I guess. Something about that window."

The two women turned simultaneously and looked at the large plate glass window at the front of the store. "It's original to the building, I think," Mae said. "Imagine all the people who have sat here, at this counter, looking through that window to check the weather or watch the world go by.

Imagine all the people who have stood outside and looked in."

Kate smiled tenderly. "You're a romantic," she said.

"I don't know about that," Mae objected. The idea made her uneasy. A lonely romantic seemed like someone who was just asking for trouble.

"You are," Kate replied, taking a sip of tea. "Takes one to know one."

Mae changed the subject. "At any rate, I am here now, aren't I? I should stop moping and get to work. That's what my mother would say."

She started to get up, but Kate held out a hand, wordlessly asking her to wait.

"I've been meaning to ask you," she said, "what happened with that detective who was looking for the book? Word around town is that he's still here and still looking. Is that right?"

"Yes." They'd come to another subject that made Mae uneasy. But since she'd talked this much, she might as well talk some more. "The other day Violet told me that she wants me to find the book and give it to the Historical Society," she confided. "I've been helping Levi look for the book, but I'm starting to feel a little guilty. If I find it, will Violet be angry if I don't give it to the town? She can be kind of…"

"Overbearing," Kate finished. "Bossy. Terrifying."

"I was going to say *strong-willed* or *determined*," Mae said, "but I guess all those terms work. I haven't even let myself think about it too much over the past few days. It seems useless to worry about it unless we find the book."

"This detective," Kate said, "you like him, don't you?"

Oh brother, this again. People loved to tease, didn't they? Well, Mae did, too, so she supposed she couldn't be too upset about it.

"Levi is a nice man," Mae replied primly. "And he takes his work very seriously. I appreciate that."

And yes, she didn't say. *I like him very much.*

"And you wouldn't want to rob him of his commission for finding the book?"

"No," Mae agreed. Especially not with his mother in the hospital.

"Then can I make a suggestion?" Kate asked. Without waiting for Mae's reply, she went on, "I happen to know someone who is very interested in preserving the history of Angel River. Why don't I see if he would be interested in acquiring this first edition Browning Weidler and donating it to the Historical Society?"

Mae's hopes began to cautiously perk up. "You mean Reed? Your husband?"

"Indeed I do," Kate replied. She popped the last bite of muffin into her mouth. "He loves buying things. I think he'd be happy to add the book to the Historical Society's inventory. Is it all right if I ask him about it?"

Mae considered. It was a generous offer, and it might solve a lot of problems. And what the heck, it was good to have options, wasn't it? If they did find the book, and if Reed was willing to match—or even exceed—Levi's client's price, wouldn't that be better for everyone?

"Sure," Mae said. "Go ahead and ask. Thanks for the offer."

Kate must have read concern on Mae's features because she laid a hand on Mae's arm. "Don't worry, I won't spread the idea all over town. I'll talk to Reed... and maybe Mrs. Gruening at the museum, if that's okay."

"That's fine." Mae spoke the words with confidence that she didn't feel. For some reason, she suspected this plan might cause more problems than it solved.

But she didn't have long to think about it because at that

moment the front bell clanged, and Mae turned to see Levi himself coming through the door.

She was startled by the palpable rush of happiness she felt at his presence. Something inside her seemed to light up. Her exhaustion evaporated. Her doubts disappeared. As Levi came across the dining room toward where she still sat, she saw every detail of his face with intense clarity. The shape of his cheekbones under his smooth skin, the luminosity of his brown eyes, the thick curl of his dark hair. She noticed a small acne scar under his left eye and a small freckle near his right ear. She saw that he favored his left leg and surmised an old injury. Sports? Military service? Random accident? Whatever it was, she had never observed it before.

Why now? she wondered. *Why today?*

Then she remembered his face at dinner, and his voice on the phone the night before, and she knew the answer to both those questions. She and Levi had crossed a borderline together. It had been unspoken and only blearily defined, but they had crossed it. They were no longer acquaintances, and no longer just friends. But neither were they in a position to be more to each other.

Levi was leaving as soon as he had the book. Mae couldn't let herself forget that.

Swallowing both her surge of happiness and the wave of disappointment that had followed it, Mae turned to Kate, and as Levi arrived at the counter, she introduced them.

"How did it go this morning with Wendell?" Mae asked.

Levi glanced at Kate then gave a facial shrug, apparently deciding that by this time, the whole town must know who he was and what he was looking for.

"He didn't have the book," Levi replied, accepting the cup of coffee that Mae held out for him. "But he did give me his copy of the estate inventory, and he mentioned something that might be worth pursuing. He said that Abe Stein had hired a man named Carl to do some carpentry on your house, and to put in what he called 'crazy hiding places.'"

"The secret compartments that Violet mentioned," Mae said excitedly. There was the Nancy Drew feeling again.

Levi nodded. "Could very well be. Do you know who Carl is?"

Kate spoke up. "Everyone in town knows Carl. He's a great guy. He and his sister, Janet, run a foster home called Haven House. Would you like me to call him for you?"

"Do you think he'd be willing to talk to us about the work he did for Mr. Stein?" Levi asked.

Kate shrugged. "Never hurts to ask."

CHAPTER 15

*A*nd indeed, it didn't. Kate called Carl on the spot, and he agreed to meet Mae and Levi at Mae's house that very evening.

"He seemed happy to help," Kate said when she got off the phone. "I think he has a soft spot for you, Mae. Men love a woman who can cook." She turned to Levi and asked pointedly, "Isn't that right, Mr. Morales?"

Startled, Levi turned a bright shade of red. He took a long drink of coffee as he tried to recover his professional demeanor. Finally, he replied, "If they don't, they should." Then he smiled. "And call me Levi, Mrs. Fitzgerald."

LEVI LEFT THE CAFÉ SHORTLY PAST NOON, AFTER INDULGING IN a bowl of beef and barley soup with a side of crusty bread. As he was leaving, the waitress named Trina pressed some oversized sugar cookies into his hand. Jeez. If he lived in Angel River, he'd have to go to the gym every day to offset the calorie intake.

If he lived in Angel River...

Thoughts like that made him nervous. This town and its citizenry—one citizen, in particular—were far too appealing. He almost felt ready to find a realtor and put down a deposit.

Except, of course, he couldn't do that. His family and his obligations were all in Hepner, Wyoming.

Speaking of which, he should call his sister and check up on his mother. But he was afraid to make that call, afraid of receiving news he wasn't ready to hear. He knew his time in Virginia was coming to an end. If he didn't find the book today, he would probably have to give up and head home tomorrow.

He prayed that Carl would be able to show them where Abel Stein had hidden that book.

Feeling restless and worried, Levi found himself driving aimlessly through the town of Angel River. Pretty country here. Beautiful, really. The land was dressed in grays and browns, the solemn attire of the winter season. And yet, even amongst this barren palette, there were surprising bursts of color, both man-made and natural. Rainbow strands of Christmas lights. The bright red of a cardinal on an old wood fence. The faded colors of a seven-pointed star on an old barn.

Impulsively, Levi tapped the brakes and pulled over. He rolled to a gentle stop, then put the car in park. The barn sat a distance from the road, rising from the frozen ground in a way that might once have been majestic, but which now just looked tired. The barn was old, its red paint mostly chipped away. The multi-colored star painted at its peak, which had caught his eye from the road, was plainly visible from this angle. Although its colors had faded, when viewed against the gray day and the grayer wood, the hues stood out, shining almost like beacons.

Levi had been in the area long enough to know that the star represented the seven days of creation and was part of the Dutch folklore known locally as Ha-la. He found such symbols, and the history behind them, to be fascinating. He got out of the car and walked toward the barn. Its roof cut a sharp angle against the ashen sky, and he thought he heard crows cawing in the eaves as wind whispered past him. Winter grass crunched under his feet.

When he reached the barn doors, he glanced around, feeling furtive. Technically, he was trespassing. But there were no signs to warn him off, it was broad daylight, and the locals had been friendly so far. He expected that if someone saw him and was angry enough to gun him down, they'd at least provide the courtesy of a warning shot first.

Levi pushed open the door and peered inside. What he saw pulled him forward as if he was on rails.

On the north-facing wall, high up by the ceiling, was a painted mural. It was a simple design, roughly drawn and shaded with swaths of color. It shouldn't have been affecting, shouldn't have captured Levi's attention or captivated his imagination. And yet it did. In that first instant of seeing it, it did.

It was so big that he couldn't take in the whole thing at once. He focused on a section of it, which stretched up to the hayloft. That part showed a tall tree, branches bare and spread wide. On one limb sat a bird, painted a crude blue, with an orange underbelly. There was writing underneath, but he couldn't make it out from this distance.

Levi took a step forward, and the floor gave a warning groan. At that moment, a voice split the air.

"You there," the voice called. It was female and carried the rasp of age, but the tone was commanding.

Levi turned his head and through the open barn door he

saw an elderly woman in a long blue coat, marching in his direction with a decidedly irritated look on her face.

When he caught her eye, she doubled her both her pace and her volume. "Get out of there. This is private property, and the structure is unsound."

Levi came obligingly out of the barn, keeping his hands at his sides and doing his best to look like the least dangerous person in the world. The woman was elderly, it was true, but her expression appeared as threatening as any weapon that Levi had encountered, and something told him that he did not want to get on this woman's bad side. At least, not any more than he apparently already was.

"I'm sorry, ma'am," he said politely. "I was just…"

What? Looking inside a stranger's barn for no good reason whatsoever?

The woman came to a halt about six feet away from him and crossed her arms, waiting to hear what excuse he was going to make for himself.

"Well, I don't know exactly what I was doing," Levi confessed meekly. "Acting like a darn fool, I suppose."

She broke into a laugh at those words—a laugh that she quickly stifled, probably not wanting to look like a pushover.

"At least you can admit it," she snapped. "What's your name, young man?"

"Levi Morales, ma'am," he said. "I'm from out of town. I'm—"

"Looking for that Weidler book." She slitted her eyes at his surprised expression. "Yes, I know all about it. I work with the Historical Society, and we've been keeping an eye on you since you got here."

Levi had to bite back a laugh. He had a sudden image of a troop of blue-haired ladies, watching him through binoculars while muttering to each other on walkie-talkies.

"Well, I'm flattered to have earned your attention. I didn't think I was that interesting," he said. "Do you mind if I ask your name?"

"Of course not. It's Gruening. Mrs. Darcia Gruening. And I have to tell you, Mr. Morales, that you're not going to find what you're looking for."

CHAPTER 16

*C*arl arrived at Mae's house promptly at six p.m. She was ready for him, with a platter of cookies, a pot of coffee and a pitcher of iced tea all laid out in the living room. Kate's visit to the café had given Mae a taste for tea, and she'd already poured herself a glass.

She'd hoped that Levi would arrive before Carl so that they could get straight what they wanted to ask him. But Levi had left during the height of the lunch rush, and Mae hadn't had a chance to say goodbye. She'd sent Trina after him with some cookies for dessert, feeling like a stereotype but unable to help herself. She was a middle-aged woman who liked to feed people sweets. Lame, perhaps, but true.

Carl didn't appear to mind, however. His face lit up when he saw the spread that Mae had prepared.

Mae hung his coat in the closet and invited him to sit, pointing out the chair he was likely to find most comfortable. He took her suggestion, and when he was sitting, she asked him if he preferred tea or coffee. He asked for the latter.

Carl was in somewhere in his late sixties or early seventies. He was small but still muscular, owing to all the gardening and repair work he did on a daily basis. He moved with a slight limp, his hair and beard were gray, but the light in his eyes belied his age.

"Thanks for coming over." Mae poured the coffee and passed it to him,

"Of course," he said. "You were so supportive when Glory was having her troubles earlier this year. I don't think I ever thanked you properly."

Mae was surprised at the sentiment. Carl's foster daughter Glory had indeed gone through some "troubles" during the course of the year. Mae hadn't done anything special besides make food and take it to the house a few times.

"Well I don't know that I did anything worthy of thanks," Mae smiled, "but I appreciate the sentiment, and I was happy to help. How's Glory doing now?"

A proud grin broke out over the man's face. "She's just finished her first semester of community college. She's still insisting that she wants to join the navy, but Janet and I have asked her to hold off a year to make sure it's really what's best for her."

Mae was quietly exhilarated to hear the good news. Glory was well known around town as a force to be reckoned with, and it was nice to know that she was channeling her energy into something positive. It gave Mae hope for the future. "Wow. She certainly has worked hard and come a long way, hasn't she?"

"Indeed, she has."

"And you and Janet worked hard to help her," Mae added. "It's commendable." She put some cookies on a plate and handed them to Carl, then glanced at the clock and held her breath, willing Levi to walk through the door. When he didn't, she inquired after Glory's sister, Chelsea, and Carl's sister, Janet.

Carl caught Mae up on all the family goings-on and then shifted around, sneaking a glance at his watch. He saw Mae looking at him and said quickly, "I'm sorry to be rude, and I don't mean to rush you. It's just that Chelsea is expecting me to help her with her homework tonight."

"No, it's okay. I don't mean to keep you."

Mae sighed, wondering where Levi was. Well, she supposed they would just have to begin without him. She had just started to explain what she was looking for when Levi finally arrived, striding breathlessly into the living room.

At his entrance, Carl rose to his feet and turned toward Levi in a motion that was both polite and slightly protective. Levi halted, understanding the body language.

"I'm sorry I didn't knock," he said quickly. "I felt bad for being so late, and when I realized that your door was unlocked, I just barged right in."

"It's fine." Mae also stood, and introduced the men.

"Oh," Carl said. "You're that fellow who's looking for the Weidler book, aren't you? Well, no wonder you want to know about Abe's hidey-holes. I'll be happy to show you what I can, although I don't know that you'll find anything in there."

"That's all right," Levi said.

He turned to Mae and opened his mouth, then closed it again. His expression was grave.

She reached out a hand as if to touch him. "Are you okay?" she asked. "Did you find out something?"

His eyes held her face. She knew she was flushed, excited. Carl had said "Abe's hidey-holes." That meant that the book could still be here, in the house.

Finally, Levi seemed to come to a decision. He nodded, briskly. "It can wait."

"Okay." Satisfied, Mae turned eagerly toward Carl. "So you did build secret compartments for Mr. Stein inside this house?"

"That I did." Carl's eyes twinkled. "It was the most interesting job I've ever been hired for, that's for certain."

They were in the home stretch now. Mae could feel it. She told Carl to lead the way.

The first thing he showed them was the safe in the bedroom closet. Mae felt like a fool for missing it when she'd searched so carefully after Violet told her about it. But then again, it was very cleverly hidden, having two separate pressure points that needed to be released simultaneously to reveal the compartment in which the safe had been sunk.

The safe itself was unlocked. And, to their chagrin, it was completely empty.

Carl then proceeded to show them two more hidden pigeonholes, which were also empty.

"So clever," Mae remarked, trying to hide her disappointment. She looked at Levi and saw heartache etched in every line of his face.

Mae sighed. "I really thought the book might still be here, in my house."

Levi opened his mouth and closed it again.

"Don't despair yet," Carl said. "There's one left. And it's my favorite. Follow me."

To Mae's surprise, Carl led them back into the living room, walking straight to the built-in bookshelves. In a single smooth motion, brushing aside Levi's offer of assistance, Carl cleared a stack of books off the shelf and set them out of the way, on the other side of the room. Then he returned to the bookshelf and reached toward the back wall.

"Abe designed this one himself. It's a pretty simple mechanism," Carl said. "But it's well hidden."

He pushed something, or he pulled something. Mae

wasn't sure which. The only thing she knew for certain was that there was a crunching sound, and then the bookshelf popped away from the wall. It was only a little opening, but Carl wedged his fingers inside and pulled—it was definitely a pull this time—until an entire section of the wall seemed to come away. The right side receded while the left side came toward them, rotating outward on a central pivot.

"Just like *Young Frankenstein*," Levi marveled, momentarily pulled out of his funk. Then he looked embarrassed. "Sorry. Did I just spoil the wonder of the moment?"

"No." Mae flashed him a quick, excited smile. "I was thinking the same thing."

When that segment of the bookcase was perpendicular to the wall, Mae squinted, trying to see into the darkness that lay beyond. If movies had taught her anything, it was that the space behind the wall should be lined with old stone and should lead downward into a deep, dark passage.

But that fantasy was quickly extinguished when Carl flipped on his flashlight and shone it inside. Behind the wall was a small chamber, maybe five feet on a side. It was lined with wood paneling, like something out of the seventies.

"Mae, if you can bring me a light bulb and a short ladder, I can get some better light in there for you." Carl flicked the beam upward, illuminating a bare-bulbed socket from which dangled a long string. "I was going to put a switch in here," he muttered. "But Abe said that was too much trouble."

"I'll get the bulb and the ladder," Levi said. He slipped away before Mae could ask him if he even knew where to find those things in her house.

But the question was forgotten as Carl stepped into the hidden room and swung the light around. After a moment's hesitation, Mae followed him.

She expected the inside to be musty and oppressive, but

instead the air was rich and sweet. Carl patted the wall. "Cedar," he explained. "And see?"

He pointed the flashlight toward the floor, where there was an air vent. "Well ventilated."

"How is it possible that I never knew this room was here?" Mae asked, turning around to follow the arc of his light. "The layout of this house isn't that complicated."

Carl shrugged. "Don't beat yourself up. You've got your guest room there, right?" He hooked a thumb to his left then nodded to the right. "Laundry room on that side. This little nook was just tucked in between, all snug and happy."

"To what purpose?"

"Abe said he was going to put some of his more valuable books in here, but it doesn't look like that ever happened." Carl shrugged. "Abe was always long on ideas but short on follow-through."

"He followed through long enough to get this room built, though," Mae murmured.

"True enough."

Carl ran the flashlight up and down the walls, moving in a slow circle. Mae was just wishing that Levi would hurry up with that ladder, and wondering if she should go help him find it, when something caught her eye.

"Wait." She reached out and touched Carl on the shoulder then held out her hand in a wordless request for the flashlight. "May I?"

He handed it to her, and she swung it to the spot where she thought she had seen something. Were her eyes playing tricks on her?

She caught her breath. No, that was no trick.

Mae stepped forward and bent down. Near the floor, in the southern corner of the little room, was a drawing. It was primitively done, not really more than a few lines, curving and intersecting at important points.

Carl crouched down and squinted. "It's a bird," he said.

Behind them, Levi's voice corrected, "It's a bluebird."

Mae turned and saw that he was standing in the doorway of the little room, with her stepping stool in one hand and a light bulb in the other. "Sorry it took me so long," he said. "Ruby insisted that I spend some time petting her."

"Yeah, she'll do that." Mae tried to ignore the little skip in her heartbeat at the way Levi spoke Ruby's name, as if he and the cat had truly bonded. What was so appealing about a man who loved cats? Brushing aside the thought, she turned back to the drawing. "You know what this is?"

He came in a little closer, and Carl stepped back so Levi could get a better look. "I've seen it before," Levi said.

"What?" Mae was startled. "When? Where?"

"And who's on first?" Levi joked. Then his face turned serious as he saw Mae's murderous expression. He hastened to answer her. "As a matter of fact, I saw it about an hour ago."

"And was it a similar drawing, or…"

"It looked just like this one," Levi said. He leaned closer to confirm then nodded. "Almost as if they'd been drawn by the same person."

"And where did you see it?" Mae asked.

Levi straightened. "In that barn on the Old Back Road."

CHAPTER 17

*W*ell, there was only one place for them to go at that point, wasn't there? Although it was fully dark by that time, Mae and Levi got into her car and headed toward the barn on Old Back Road.

They had invited Carl to come with them, but he begged off, reminding Mae about Chelsea and his homework duties. He wished them luck on their adventure, and he told them to let him know how things turned out.

As she drove, Levi explained how he had found the barn, and what he'd seen when he'd looked inside. He wound up his story, then hesitated, and added, "There's something else you should know, Mae. I'm leaving town tomorrow morning."

Something small and fluffy ran out into the road. Mae swerved, missing it by inches. Heart pounding, she braked hard and pulled off to the side of the road, where the gravel petered out and was replaced by sharp, stubby winter grass.

She put the car in park and turned to look at Levi. She'd known this moment would come, of course, but she'd become so fond of him that she'd managed to convince herself that their parting would be days away, maybe even weeks. Now she knew it was only a matter of hours.

Mae pressed her trembling lips together and asked the only question that mattered. "Did something happen with your mother?"

"It's not that." He reached out and took her hand. Neither of them was wearing gloves, though the night was more than cold enough to warrant it. This was the first time he had touched her, she realized, and she willed herself to remember every detail of the moment—how the moonlight slanted in and laid a silver finger on his chin, the shape of him next to her, the way he smelled, and the good roughness of his hand encircling hers. Their cold fingers warmed with contact, and they sat that way for several long moments, silently drawing heat from one another.

Finally, Levi spoke again. "My mother is still in the hospital, and her prognosis hasn't changed. The doctors think she's old and weak. She thinks she's old and strong. My sister is a nervous wreck. And I need to be there, not here."

"But the book—"

"Might not be for me to find," he interrupted gently.

Mae couldn't stand that idea. She simply couldn't stand it. Levi had come all this way, had invested so much time and attention to finding the book. And she'd gotten emotionally involved, hadn't she? Not just with Levi, but with his—his *quest*, for lack of a more grown-up word. She wanted to find that book as much as he did. Then she remembered his face when he'd entered her house earlier. What was going on?

"You were going to tell me something before," Mae said slowly, "and I put you off."

Levi sighed heavily. "Yes. Earlier today when I was at the barn, I met Mrs. Gruening."

Mae blinked. "Oh," she said. "Well, I guess that makes sense. She owns it."

"She came at me with both barrels blazing, although I managed to win her over in the end."

"Of course you did." Mae smiled.

"But she told me flat out that I wouldn't find what I was looking for. She said that Abe Stein was quite mad by the time he died, and he most likely destroyed the book."

"I don't believe that," Mae burst out. "When you love something as much as he loved that book…"

She didn't know how to finish. Levi spoke into the silence. "Wendell Beaufort told me basically the same thing as Mrs. Gruening. Both said that Abel Stein's mental faculties had declined sharply during his last years of life, and that whatever he did with that book, I'd likely never find it."

Mae went quiet again. Her sadness was too deep for words.

"So why are we going out to the barn?" She asked. "Why even bother?"

He squeezed her hand. "Because I want to show you that wonderful drawing. I want us to get close enough to read the words that are painted underneath. I want us to have one last adventure together before we go our separate ways."

Mae smiled sadly. One last adventure together. It wasn't nearly what either of them had hoped for, but at least it was something.

"Okay," she said. "Let's go."

She put the car in drive and pulled back out onto the road.

ALTHOUGH THEY'D LEFT MAE'S HOUSE IN A HURRY, THEY'D made sure to bring two flashlights with them. When they reached the barn, Mae parked, removed the torches from the back seat, and locked her purse in the trunk before they made their way toward the structure that loomed ahead of them, dark and silent in the night.

"I hope nobody's in the mood to shoot trespassers," Mae said suddenly. "I mean, folks out here are friendly and all, but two random people with flashlights might—"

"Call attention in a bad way?" Levi smiled. "I asked Mrs. Gruening about that earlier. When she came up on me, I half expected her to whip a shotgun out from under her coat."

Mae couldn't help but laugh at the image. "And what did she say?"

"That chances of being shot were slim to none. If someone gets nervous, they'll call the police. They won't take the law into their own hands without provocation."

"Well, I've never been arrested," she replied, "so that might be something new and exciting."

"Exciting doesn't precisely cover it," Levi said. He caught Mae's look and smiled disarmingly.

Suddenly, Mae's heart felt light as a feather. And why not? True, this was a somber occasion, but it was also an adventure. An adventure with her tall, dark, handsome stranger, on a quest for a rare and magical book. This kind of situation didn't exactly happen to her every day. She decided it was okay if she enjoyed it, at least a little bit.

The barn door opened easily, and they shone their flashlights on the floor, being careful of weak spots in the planks. Levi led her forward into the darkness, his torch cutting a pathway through the gloom.

"The mural is over here," he said. "Way up high."

He pointed the flashlight, and Mae gasped. The mural was huge, covering most of the wall. It was too much for her to take in all at once, so she let Levi's light guide her eyes and focused on the part of the painting that he pointed out to her. It was indeed a bluebird, exactly like the one in her closet.

"Wow," Mae breathed. She wished she could take pictures,

but her phone camera would never pick up the fine detailing the way she would want to, especially not in this gloom. She'd have to tell Donaghy about this place so he could come back with his iPhone in the daylight. Or maybe he'd want to go crazy and use an actual camera.

"I know." Levi stood very close to her, his presence warm and reassuring in the dark. "And look at that."

He moved his light so it shone on a ribbon of words that seemed to curl around the far edge of the design.

"Oh." Mae swung her own torch and traced the lines of the barn until she found an ancient hayloft then went farther until she found the ladder leading up to it. "Better vantage point up there," she said. "Should we take a closer look?"

"I'm not sure it's a good idea for us to go climbing through an old building in the middle of the night."

"Come on," Mae prodded. "Are we on an adventure here, or aren't we?"

"Yes, but I don't want either of us to end up in a cast or getting a round of tetanus shots."

That image brought her up short, but she brushed off her worry. "We'll be careful," she assured him. "Come on, let's at least scope it out."

The ladder looked relatively sturdy. Levi said, "I'll go up first and make sure it'll take my weight. Then you can come up, and we'll get closer to that inscription." His face brightened as something seemed to occur to him. "Or better yet, we can come back tomorrow, in the daylight. I don't have to leave first thing in the morning, you know."

"No," Mae said. "Let's do it now. We can argue later about your time of departure."

Cheeky, she said to herself. *Calm down, pushy.*

But she couldn't. Her blood was up, and she didn't think she would sleep tonight until she'd read that inscription, whatever it was. And there was a tiny, childish part of her that felt certain she needed to read the words written on that wall. She and Levi had come so far, she wanted—*needed*—for the words to be something special for the two of them. Common sense had fled, and in its place was only the driving urgency to pull something meaningful from the melee of the past few days.

Levi studied her for a long moment, then he sighed. "Fine," he said. "But I'm going up first, okay?"

Having won the war, she consented to lose the battle. She stepped to the side, grasping the ladder firmly as he began to climb. He tried each rung before he put his weight on it, ascending slowly and carefully. He was halfway to the top when a sinister splintering sound shot through the night. Mae felt the ladder crumble under her hands, and Levi dropped like a stone.

"Levi!" Mae cried, but it was much too late for warnings. He plunged downward and slammed into the floor, which cracked under his weight. For a single, terrifying instant, Mae felt the whole barn shudder and was sure it was going to collapse in on them. She wanted to rush to Levi, to see if he was all right. But she stood still, afraid that a movement in any direction might hasten the cave-in.

Suddenly, a voice cut through her fear. "Mae Wallace!" The voice thundered. "What are you doing in there? Come out here immediately!"

Mae turned and saw Mrs. Gruening standing behind them, a flashlight of her own in her hand.

WITH THE APPEARANCE OF MRS. GRUENING, MAE'S SENSES returned and with them came the crushing awareness of how badly Levi might have been hurt as a result of her careless demands.

Thankfully, he didn't seem to have suffered any serious

injury, although he did wince when she accidentally touched his knee. Mae helped him to his feet, and he leaned on her as they shuffled out of the barn, hanging their heads like abashed children.

Mrs. Gruening was waiting for them, her lips compressed into a tight line. "I can't believe you, Mae. I thought you were smarter than this. And *you!*" She rounded on Levi. "Didn't I just chase you out of here, not two hours ago? What are you thinking? I have a good mind to call the police and report you both."

Instead of doing that, however, she went to Levi's other side and put a supporting arm around him. Together, she and Mae helped him toward the car. Mae opened the door, and Levi settled inside, wincing slightly as he adjusted his left leg.

Mrs. Gruening said, "I won't even ask you what you were doing here tonight. I have a feeling that no matter what you say, I'll be fairly disgusted."

"We came to get a better look at the mural inside the barn," Levi told her. "I saw it when I was here earlier today, and then when I went to Mae's house, we found a bluebird drawn inside a secret room that looked exactly like the one in there."

Mrs. Gruening didn't reply immediately. She just stood blinking owlishly. Finally, she said, "A secret room inside Mae's house."

There was no verbal question mark at the end of that sentence, and yet a question had definitely been posed. It was: *Do you take me for a dang fool?*

"I know it sounds crazy," Levi said, "but it's the God's honest truth. Who painted that mural in your barn? Was it Abe Stein?"

"Those drawings have been here for decades," Mrs. Gruening said. "I have no idea who painted them, but I sincerely doubt it was Abel Stein. If you're still following breadcrumbs and hoping to find that book, Mr. Morales, you've been led in the wrong direction."

"I'm not being led anywhere," Levi replied, somewhat testily. "The only thing I'm following is a line of inquiry."

"I told you earlier that the book is long gone. It's sheer folly to keep looking for it. And that's a shame," Mrs. Gruening added, turning to Mae, "because Reed told me that he would have been glad to buy the book if you had found it."

"What?" Levi asked, visibly confused. "What are you talking about?"

Mae sagged. She hadn't meant for Levi to find out this way. Of course, it was irrelevant now, but still, it was a kind of betrayal to go behind his back like that, wasn't it? "I have something to confess," she said.

With that, Mrs. Gruening rolled her eyes. "And this is where I make my exit," she said. "I have no desire to be privy to lovers' confessions in the dark of night."

Mae was about to correct Mrs. Gruening's impression of her relationship with Levi, when a more pressing matter came to mind.

"What about the words written on the design?" she asked, before Mrs. Gruening could leave them. "What do they say?"

Mrs. Gruening hesitated. "I'm not sure I should tell you. You both seem in the mood to make a lot out of nothing."

"Please," Mae said. "I just want to know."

"Fine," Mrs. Gruening relented. Then she quoted, "'Oh winged spirit, who from on high descends. Pity, save us from our mortal ends.'"

Levi's mouth dropped open.

"Why is that important?" Mae asked. "What does it mean?"

He looked at her but could not speak.

Mrs. Gruening answered for him. "It's a quote from *The Book of Forgotten Angels*."

. . .

DESPITE MRS. GRUENING'S ASSERTION THAT SHE WAS GOING to leave them, she stayed on site long enough to make sure Mae was safely back in her car with the engine started. Then Mrs. Gruening drove off, taillights winking at them in the nighttime.

"I guess we have some things to talk about," Mae said.

"I guess we do," Levi replied. There was no accusation in his words, just exhausted resignation.

Mae sighed heavily and explained. "When Kate came into the café earlier, we ended up talking about the book. I told her that Violet Morrow had pressured me to give it to the Historical Society if we found it in my house, but I didn't want to come between you and your job. So Kate suggested that maybe Reed would pay for the book. I'm sorry," she added. "I know you have an obligation to your client, and I should have consulted you before I let Kate talk to Reed. But everything happened so fast, and—"

"Oh, Mae." Levi leaned back against the seat and closed his eyes.

"Are you really angry?" She hadn't expected that.

"Not angry at all," he replied. "I don't have the right to be angry with you about anything."

"What do you mean?"

"I mean that there *is* no client," Levi said. "*I'm* the client."

Mae sank back. "Wow," she murmured. "Then I guess we really do have some things to talk about."

"Yeah," Levi said. "I guess we really do."

CHAPTER 18

*H*e talked while she drove. His words seemed to come very quickly, as though he'd been saving them up for a long time.

"The first thing you should know," he began, "is that my mother's name is Hope Roebeck. She's the woman who wrote the biography of Browning Weidler."

"Really?" Mae's first reaction was pure delight. "That's so cool." Then the other shoe dropped. "But why didn't you tell me that earlier?"

"Because I was embarrassed. This trip... it's an act of contrition, Mae. I'm trying to repay my mother, to make up for something she lost because of my recklessness."

Mae waited, knowing he would continue. Outside the car, the darkness embraced them on all sides, broken only by her headlights and the occasional flash of yellow light through an uncovered house window. The stillness felt complete, as if the whole world was waiting to hear Levi's story.

He sighed as he began. "My mother was the one who bought that book at auction in 1983, not Abe Stein. It was her pride and joy. She'd always been a fan of Browning

Weidler's, and to own an autographed copy of her favorite book was the kind of riches she'd never dreamed of. My mother was a teacher, a single parent, never had two nickels to rub together. But no matter how badly she may have needed money, she could never bring herself to part with the book. Until I got arrested."

"Oh," Mae said. "How awful. For both of you."

"I didn't even had the chance to argue with her, or try to talk her out of it." Levi moved restlessly, agitated by the memory. "She sold the book, her most prized possession, to pay for my legal defense. Thanks to her, I avoided prison. She never blamed me or said a word to express how heart-broken she must have been to sell that book. But she did tell me the name of the man who bought it."

Mae breathed, feeling an absurd combination of enchant-ment and distress. "You mean—"

"The man who bought her book, the man who vicariously got me out of a prison sentence, was Abel Stein." Levi dragged a hand over his face. "I knew how much that book meant to her, and I always promised myself that I would get it back for her someday. So two weeks ago, when she went into the hospital…"

"You knew you had to make good on your promise. And you went looking for the book."

"I must have been crazy," he said. "Instead of staying in Hepner, being a good son and a good brother, I left my sister to deal with everything and took off." He buried his head in his hands. "I'm so sorry for all of this. I hurt them both. And I would have hurt you, too."

"You would never have hurt me." Mae spoke with a stout certainty that she didn't fully understand. "And grief makes us do crazy things. Look at me. I moved nine hundred miles, completely upended my life when my mother died."

"I haven't told you the worst part yet." Levi hesitated, then spoke in a rush, as if he had to say the words before he lost his nerve. "I lied to you about the money. I don't have twenty-five thousand dollars. I was going to give you the few thousand I have in my bank account, and then figure out the rest when I got home."

He pressed his lips together and shook his head, as if even he couldn't believe his own deception. "I don't know what I was thinking. I promise I would have found a way to pay you eventually. I would have sold my car, sold everything I owned…"

He trailed off. Mae digested what he had told her. It was an ugly admission, one which she couldn't reconcile with the good man she'd come to know in the past days.

"This was not a great plan," she said.

"No," he agreed fervently. "It really wasn't. And I don't expect you could ever forgive me."

"Grief makes us do crazy things." She repeated her earlier words, feeling her way through the concept in light of this new information. "If all you could see was your mother dying without ever seeing that book again…"

"Which will happen anyway," Levi said miserably. "I'm convinced that Mrs. Gruening's right. That book is long gone. Burned or buried or lying at the bottom of Angel River. All of this has been for nothing."

"That's where you're wrong," Mae stated. "It hasn't been for nothing. You and I met. We became friends. Whatever you've done before, whatever you might have done after we found the book… those things are irrelevant. We are friends. And only the future counts."

"Let's be honest, Mae. I'm a mess. You deserve better than a future with a guy like me."

Mae pulled into her driveway, rolling to a slow stop in front of her house. She was exhausted. She was hurt. She was confused. But she wasn't ready to give up.

"I'll decide what kind of future I deserve." Her voice was as firm as her resolve. "Now let's go inside. We still have work to do."

"What are you talking about?"

"I have an idea," she told him. "I want to have one more go at finding the book."

"I've decided two things," Mae told him.

They were in the kitchen. Levi had put on a pot of coffee, which was currently brewing. And at Mae's request, he had pulled Wendell's copy of the estate inventory out of his car. It currently lay on the kitchen table, next to the book inventory that Mae had made that first day they'd met. Had that really only been four days ago? Seemed impossible.

"The first thing I've decided," Mae continued, "is that Abe Stein wanted someone to find that book. His mental faculties may have been deteriorated, but he still would have wanted that book to go to someone who would love it as much as he did. So the book is out there somewhere, waiting for someone to find it."

Levi wished he could believe that as strongly as Mae did, but he was willing to keep looking for a little bit longer, if it made her happy.

"The second thing I've decided," Mae said, "is that the only clues that Abe left behind were things in this house."

"Why?" Levi asked, surprised.

"Well, think about it. Everyone said he was a recluse. He hardly ever left this place." She laid a hand on each set of papers in front of her. "The answer must be on these lists somewhere. I'm going to compare the attorney's inventory with mine. Something's got to shake loose."

"I guess it never hurts to look," Levi said, pulling mugs from the cabinet. "I'll keep the coffee going."

"Good."

Levi couldn't believe she was still in this, still swinging away, especially since she knew how he had lied to her. She smiled at him then bent her glossy head over the paperwork.

"Wait a minute." She looked up. There was a gleam in her eye. "Oh my God."

"What?" Was it possible she had actually found something? And so soon?

"It's the first thing I looked for, and it's not here," she whispered.

"What?" he repeated.

She motioned him over, and he went to look at the two sets of papers laid out in front of her. She tapped her list. "This one, right here," she said. "This one is not on the estate inventory."

He leaned closer. *A Guide to Field Identification of Birds of North America.*

"Is it a fluke?" he asked. "There were a ton of books in your shed. Surely it was a mistake that the assessor made when he didn't put that one down. I mean, do you really think it means something?"

She was still looking at him. He laughed nervously. "What?"

She quoted, "'Oh winged spirit who from on high descends. Pity, save us from our mortal ends.' That's what it said in the barn, right? And there was a picture of a bluebird there, and one in that nook behind the bookshelf?"

"Right." Levi said slowly.

Mae stood up. "Come with me."

She took his hand, wrapped it in her warm fingers, and led him into the living room. There, from the very shelf that Carl had opened not three hours before, she pulled out a book. The dust jacket was faded, painted with three birds. One of them was a bluebird.

With trembling fingers, she removed the dust jacket. The book underneath was plain, almost homely, covered in unassuming brown cloth. It could be anything, this book. It could be anything—or nothing.

Levi held his breath as Mae carefully opened the cover.

There, on the title page, were the words they'd needed to see.

The Book of Forgotten Angels
Copyright 1899
First printing

And in faded, sprawling handwriting, there was an inscription: "To a young man with a bright future. May it come sooner rather than later." It was signed "Browning Weidler."

CHAPTER 19

ABEL STEIN, 2002

When the whispers stopped coming, Abe knew he was going to die.

Funny thing, that. He'd always thought that imminent death would make him frantic, but when it came right down to it, he wasn't at all sad about shuffling off his mortal coil. Truth be told, his time on this earth had served no purpose whatsoever. What had he done, after all? He'd made a lot of money, seen his friends die overseas, killed some men that had had called "enemy" but who in fact had only been scared kids, like himself.

Abe wasn't sad to die. And he wasn't frantic. He just figured it was about time.

But before he died, he had some work to do, didn't he? He needed to save his book. *The* book. The one that young-old Hope had handed him with such trembling fingers only a few years before. But who could he give it to? Who would treasure it, value it, give it the care it needed?

With growing desperation, Abe began to cast about for the book's new caretaker. Mr. Forrester? No, he decided.

Forrester was nice enough but wouldn't recognize that the real value of the book was in its soul.

Wendell? No, again. Wendell might have been Abe's best friend, but he couldn't be trusted with a pack of white mice, never mind a prize like *Forgotten Angels.*

Who did that leave? Violet? Carl? The kid who delivered Abe's groceries every week? No, no, and no.

The only person worthy enough to take care of this book, Abe realized, was young-old Hope herself. He had seen the way she'd looked at it, had known how dearly it had cost her to part with it. He felt certain that the book would find its way back to her one day.

With that resolved, he merely needed to figure out where to put the book until it could be reunited with her again.

And so had begun the series of secret compartments that Carl had installed in Abe's house. The process had been slow and strange, for Abe's hold on reality had indeed started to slip. He would have Carl make what seemed like the perfect niche, only to realize that none of them were right.

Couldn't put the book under the floor. What if there was a flood?

Couldn't put the book behind the paneling. Wasn't that the first place burglars would look?

Couldn't put the book in the secret room behind the bookshelf. The room was too big. It made the book look small and insignificant.

Finally, finally, he had figured out what to do. Years ago, he had, as it were, seen the writing on the wall. "Winged spirit," indeed. There were many kinds of winged spirits, weren't there? Not just angels.

And so he'd taken the dust jacket off his old birding book and wrapped it snuggly around the book of angels. It fit, warm and perfect, like an embrace. The actual bird book had gone into the fire.

Abe had never considered himself much use to God or man. But all that had changed the day he'd first seen *The Book of Forgotten Angels.*

He adjusted the cover slightly and tucked the book onto the shelf.

Safe, he told himself. *Safe, until Hope can find it. Or until it finds her.*

CHAPTER 20

DECEMBER 2007

Levi

The Book of Forgotten Angels lay on Mae's kitchen table, looking very large on the small surface. Mae and Levi sat silently, just gazing at it. They had been sitting that way for nearly half an hour. Neither of them was sure what to do next. They were almost afraid to touch it.

Ruby, however, had no such compunctions. She jumped repeatedly onto the table, nuzzling the book, insisting on being a part of the action—or inaction, in this case. Every time she did this, Mae would absentmindedly pick up the cat and attempt to cradle her. Ruby would squawk her objection, slither onto the floor, then circle the kitchen, waiting for her chance to return to the table.

After this sequence had recurred for the fourth time, Levi took the cat and placed her in his own lap. She settled down immediately, twisting in feline joy as he stroked her. Mae just shook her head.

Finally, Levi spoke. "I can't believe it was here the whole time."

When he heard the words, he was embarrassed by their inanity. He should have something more poetic to say in this moment of moments.

"If only I had looked more at the bird book more closely," Mae replied apologetically. "I could have saved you so much trouble."

"Hey." The word came softly as Levi caught her gaze and held it. "I'm the one who's caused you trouble. And in spite of everything, this is the most fun I've had in ages."

"Me too." She smiled sadly.

They fell quiet again.

He wished he could spin out this time, this moment of quiet awe and mystery, with the two of them sitting there, contemplating the book. It was like holding his breath, watching a slowly revolving compass needle that had yet to point the way north. When the needle fell still, would it direct him and Mae toward each other—or away?

Well, there was only one answer to that question. He was out of time, and out of choices.

Without thinking, Levi reached over and took Mae's hand. She squeezed back, and he felt the warmth of her flesh, the rightness of her presence in his life. He lifted his eyes to meet hers and found she was looking at him tenderly, with complete understanding. He knew that the time had come to break the silence. The compass had found its direction.

"The book is yours," he said. "Keep it, or give it away, or sell it if you like. You found it. It belongs to you."

"No," she said. "You should take it for your mother."

"I can't pay you," he said painfully.

"I don't—"

"Don't say you don't care about the money," he begged. "You were going to do good things with that money, remember? You talked about giving bonuses to your staff, making a donation to the food bank. And you can still do that. You can still sell the book to the town, let them keep it for the Historical Society."

He took a breath. "My search for this book was a way to avoid responsibility to my mother. But she doesn't need a book. She needs her son. And my sister needs her brother. And what I have to do now is keep my promises to them and go sit vigil at the hospital."

Mae thought for a long time. Her eyes never wavered from his face. She said, "If I sell the book, the money is going to be half yours. Your family will need it. Medical bills, and…"

Levi smiled tenderly. He adored this woman. Truly, he did. If only he were even close enough to being good for her. "My bills are not your worry. That money belongs to you, as does the book itself."

Reluctantly, he unclasped his hand from hers. "I'm going to go home and pack. I'll leave first thing in the morning."

Almost automatically, she asked. "Do you want to come by the café for coffee?" Then she blushed, as if she knew there would be no time for that.

"I wish I could," he said. "But I'll really need to hightail it westward. It's a long drive, and I'm hoping to be in Nebraska by tomorrow night. That will get me home by lunch on Friday."

"Of course," she murmured.

They stood up, and he handed over Ruby, who for once did not object to being moved without her permission. Holding the cat, Mae walked him to the door. He put on his coat and opened the door, stepped over the threshold, then turned and looked back.

Mae held Ruby in her arms, rubbing the cat's neck. Ruby's eyes were slitted in happiness. When the wintry air of the outdoors hit her, she rotated her head languidly and looked at him with glittering eyes, daring him to choose the cold darkness instead of the warmth and love that waited inside Mae's house.

He reached out his hand, wanting to stroke Mae's cheek. Instead, he ran a finger down Ruby's spine. "Bye Rube," he murmured. "Take care of our Mae."

Ruby arched under his hand, accepting as her natural right the dual worship of humans in her thrall.

Levi lifted his eyes to Mae's and wished he knew what to say. He groped for words that were true and right, words that could say everything he was feeling. But he could find none. So he just stood there, mute, awash in regret.

Finally, Mae spoke, "Drive safely. I'll call you later."

"You don't have to do that."

"I know. But I will."

He put his hand in his pocket, where it felt cold and empty. He took two steps backward, then turned, and walked down the stairs. He didn't look back.

CHAPTER 21

*E*xhausted as she was, Mae knew she had more work to do on that pitchy, bleak December night. So after Levi had driven away, she changed into clean clothes, made sure Ruby had food and water, wrapped the book in a clean hand towel, and walked out the door before she could second guess her thoughts.

She reached the café just as Trina and Donaghy were closing up. The front door was locked, the blinds were drawn, and they were stacking chairs on the tables when she walked in.

"Mae," Trina said, surprised. "We weren't expecting to see you. Is everything okay?"

In answer, she drew the book from her handbag and held it out for them to see. As they oohed and ahhed, she told them everything, in the simplest possible terms. She told them where she and Levi had found the book. She told them about the money, about Reed, and about Levi's mother.

"So the question is," Mae said, "what do we do with the book?"

She watched them look at each other, wordlessly

discussing their options. Mae's heart melted just a little. Could she ever have really felt like an outsider in this beautiful place, with these beautiful young people in her life?

This was her own little family. Regardless of what they did with their futures, regardless of where they went or whether they had families of their own, they were hers, and they always would be. Just like families, they might drift from one another, but that didn't change the fact that they were all here together now, and that was all she needed to know.

Trina spoke for both herself and Donaghy. "There's really only one answer. You give the book to Levi."

"What about the Historical Society?" Mae asked.

"Like they don't have enough old stuff in that museum already?" Trina shrugged. "They don't need it. It sounds like Levi's mother does."

"But the money," Mae objected weakly. "I was going to give it to you."

"I'm not going to steal the dream of a dying old lady just so I can pay my student loans," Donaghy said, with both the brutal frankness of a very young man, and the touching sincerity of a very old soul. He shook his cranberry-colored hair vigorously. "I don't need Reed Fitzgerald's money. I want Levi's mother to have the book."

"If you're both sure…"

They assured her that they were.

"Okay," she said. A cozy peace descended on her, like a soft wool blanket. The decision had been made, and that was that.

Donaghy had carefully turned the pages of the book back to the inscription. "This is so strangely worded." He frowned. "You have no idea who it might be written to?"

"Levi said he didn't know." Mae's blanket of peace ruffled

slightly as she realized anew that Levi was leaving town in the morning.

Trina, having no way to know what Mae was feeling, exhaled a long, happy breath. "Another puzzle." She seemed to like the idea. "It's so great. Who wants to know everything? I like a little mystery in my life. It makes things more interesting."

In spite of her sadness, Trina's words made Mae smile. Her eyes twinkled as she said, "You're a romantic."

"Ugh." Trina wrinkled her nose. "Perish the thought."

"You are," Mae insisted. Recalling her conversation with Kate, she sighed and added, "It takes one to know one."

CHAPTER 22

*M*ae was at Levi's motel before dawn the
following day. She had almost gone to see
him on the previous night, but something told her that if she
knocked on his door in the wee small hours, she wouldn't
make it home again. And she simply wasn't strong enough to
make love with him and then watch him drive away.

Even now, Mae didn't trust herself to get out of the car,
imagining Levi still warm from sleep, the bed covers tousled
and inviting. And so she watched through her windshield
and waited for him to emerge into the cold morning air.

Finally, his door opened, and he came out, with an
ancient duffel bag slung over his shoulder. Mae picked up the
book, which she had carefully wrapped in brown paper and
tied with twine. Underneath the paper, the book was still
nestled inside the dust jacket of *A Guide to Field Identification
of Birds of North America*. Somehow the two belonged
together.

Mae got out of the car and moved forward. Gravel
crunched under her feet. Levi's head turned at the sound.
When he saw her, he paused in the act of closing his motel

room door. Then he slowly pulled it shut behind him. His eyes went from her face to the package in her hand and back again.

He took several steps in her direction and met her halfway. "Mae—"

She knew what he was going to say. "You're taking the book," she interrupted. "No arguments, no denials. You're doing what you came here to do. You're taking this book to your mother."

"Trina and Donaghy—"

"They agree with me completely."

She pressed the package into his hands. His gloved fingers closed around hers, and they stood very close together, holding the book between them. Mae felt him begin to argue, then abruptly give in.

"Thank you." His voice trembled. "I'm taking this for my mother, not for myself."

"I know." She raked his face with her gaze, wanting to absorb every detail of his features.

"I feel guilty," he breathed. "I feel so terribly guilty. For lying to you. For lying to my family. For being here. For leaving here. I feel guilty for everything. For my mother having to sell this book in the first place."

"So?" She tilted her head. "Don't waste time with guilt. Do the hard work of making up for it. Build a life you can be proud of."

"Is it that easy?"

"No," she said frankly. "It's that hard. But it's that worth it."

He leaned his forehead against hers. "I wish I deserved to stay here, to be with you. I want to be the kind of man who could make you happy. The kind of man that you might even —even grow to love. Someday."

There it was. *Love.* The word that Mae wouldn't let

herself speak. Thank goodness he had said it first. She cleared her throat and told herself to be strong.

"You already are that kind of man. But you're going to have to find a way to let yourself believe it."

Levi leaned down, the book between them, and pressed his lips gently to hers. The contact was soft and subtle, yet full of spice and sweetness. She could smell the pine trees that stood nearby, could feel the cold that numbed her toes and made her cheeks tingle. And there was Levi, strong and warm and complicated and real. Not perfect, not some Christmas wish, but a real, live human being.

He broke the kiss and pressed his cheek against hers. "I'm glad I met you." The words were a warm sigh in her ear.

Mae asked the only question that mattered. "Will you come back to me?"

"Oh, yes," he replied. "Not even a flock of bluebirds could keep me away."

CHAPTER 23

ne of the hardest things Levi had ever done was to
let Mae go, get in his car, and drive away from
Angel River.

The road home was long, the trip monotonous. At least
he had plenty of time to think about her and about himself
and about the decisions he'd made with his life.

He stopped at that same motel in Nebraska and spent yet
another sleepless night on a lumpy mattress. He arose before
dawn, got back in his car, and headed home again.

When he arrived in Hepner, he went straight to the
hospital. He took the package from the seat beside him, ran a
hand through his hair, and got out of the car. He inquired at
the front desk and made his way through the maze of hall-
ways. And before he knew it, he was standing in front of the
open door of his mother's room.

Ruth was holding their sleeping mother's hand. When
Levi took a step inside, her head swiveled. He thought he saw
relief sweep over her face, quickly chased away by anger. Her
eyes pinned him hotly. She started to stand, then apparently
thought better of it, not wanting to wake Mom.

Ruth's mouth opened then closed again. He could see sharp and biting comments hovering right behind her lips, but Ruth wouldn't risk their mother's slumber to utter them. He was sure, however, that he would get an earful as soon as they were alone.

Without a word, Levi moved forward and took their mother's other hand. He and Ruth looked at each other over her shrunken, huddled form. Finally, the fight seemed to seep out of his younger sister. Her anger cooled, and she slumped slightly.

Levi nestled carefully on the side of the bed and gazed at his mother's face. Her curly hair had long ago gone completely gray, but her forehead was still unlined. With her face relaxed, she looked like a strange combination of child and old woman. Levi's heart felt hollow. How could he have run away and left her here? And what were he and Ruth going to do when Mom finally left them?

As if his mother could feel his gaze and hear his thoughts, her eyes fluttered open. When she focused on his face, recognition flooded her expression, and she smiled.

"Levi," she murmured, voice weak. "I was dreaming about you."

Levi saw his sister's face crumple slightly. He had always been his mother's favorite, a position that he neither sought nor deserved. Definitely not deserved.

Hope continued. "I'm so glad you're here. We've been waiting for you. Haven't we, Ruthie?"

Ruth rallied, putting on a brave and overly bright smile. "We sure have. And it looks like Levi brought you a present."

With difficulty, Hope pulled her hands back from her children. "Why are we holding hands? Are we praying? I'm not dying yet," she joked. She tried to push herself into a sitting position, and her children helped adjust her bed and pillows until she was comfortable. Then there was water to pour, and she asked for a cup of tea, which Ruth told her she could have later. Hope met this statement with a frown but didn't push to have her way.

Levi and Ruth settled again on the bed, and Hope untied the package with trembling fingers. She commented on how well it was wrapped. "So pretty. Almost like a present." At her words, Levi pictured Mae carefully tying the twine, and his heart swelled a little, remembering her presence and missing her.

As the paper fell away, Levi saw the dust jacket for the bird book. It brought back sharply the moment that Mae had pulled the book from the shelf two nights ago.

"What's this?" Hope asked. "A book on birds?"

He reached over and gently opened the cover, revealing the title page.

Hope drew a breath. "Oh my God." Her voice shook.

"What?" Ruth leaned closer to look. "Mom, what is it?" Then, with quiet awe: "Oh."

Hope's bright, round eyes found Levi's. "How—how did you find this?"

Levi explained why he had gone to Angel River and what the job had entailed. He left out some of the finer details, such as how he and Mae had come to feel about each other, but something in his mother's shrewd expression told him that she may have guessed what he was trying to hide.

"So you left us to get this book?" Ruth was obviously outraged. "You didn't even make any money on this so-called 'job'?"

"I was trying to make amends," he said quietly. "I was trying to keep my promise."

He could tell from Ruth's face that she understood why he'd done what he'd done, but that didn't take away the sting of his actions.

"You had other promises to keep too." Ruth shot the words at him. "Like the promise to be a good brother."

"Hush now, Ruth," Hope said. She was examining Browning Weidler's signature as though it was the face of a long-lost love.

"That inscription, Mom," Levi said. "What does it mean? Who is the young man?"

"I was never able to find out," Hope sighed. "Maybe it's meant for whoever needs to read it. Abe Stein. Or you. Or even me, gender notwithstanding. I like to believe I still have a bright future ahead of me, even if it's just one more day with my children."

She looked up, eyes brimming. "I can't believe you did this. I can't believe you found it for me."

"It must have cost a fortune," Ruth put in.

"It wasn't that difficult," he said to his mother. And to Ruth, he added softly, "Barely cost a penny, except for gas, of course." *And except for my heart*, he could have added. "I stayed in the cheapest motel I could find."

"Ruth, give your brother and me a few minutes alone, please," Hope said brusquely.

Ruth looked hurt, but she rose without complaint and walked out the door, murmuring something about finding that cup of tea that Hope had wanted.

"I wish you would be a little softer with her," Levi said, without thinking, as he watched his sister disappear down the hall. "All she's ever wanted is your approval."

"She's always had it," Hope said. "She's just never had the self-confidence to recognize it when it came her way."

"Maybe you should just tell her," Levi replied. "Save her the worry."

Hope's eyes twinkled. "Well, look at you, sticking up for your sister."

"I guess it's about time, huh?"

Hope didn't reply to that. Instead, she said, "Why don't you start from the beginning and tell me everything that happened on your trip—and everyone you met."

Typical Mom radar. She must have known, just by looking, that Levi had met someone.

He laughed. "Well," he said, reaching out for his mother's hand. "Her name is Mae, and she has a cat."

He told the truth, the whole truth and nothing but. By the time Ruth returned with three cups of tea and some little bags of cookies, Levi was just getting to the part of the story where Mrs. Gruening had found him and Mae in the barn after dark. Ruth sat down wordlessly and listened as he finished his tale.

"And then I got in the car and came home," Levi summed up simply.

"You just left Mae there, standing in the parking lot of your crummy motel?" Ruth asked, disbelieving. "No wonder you're still single. That woman is way too good for you."

"Don't I know it," Levi said with feeling.

"It's so amazing that you actually went to Angel River," Hope said excitedly, "the place where Browning Weidler was born."

"I can't believe you've never been there, Mom," Ruth said. "We should have taken that trip a long time ago."

"The Historical Society would love to meet you, I'm sure," Levi agreed.

Hope's hand lingered on the book. "Maybe we should plan a little something for the new year," she mused. She looked at her children. "What do you think?"

Ruth and Levi exchanged a glance. Levi could see that his sister wanted to warn their mother not to get her hopes up, that she might not be strong enough to make that trip. But Ruth fought the urge and instead said, "Any time you want to go, Mom, I'll make it work. I'd love to see Angel River with you."

Hope rested a hand briefly against her daughter's cheek. "You're a good girl, Ruth."

Levi had to turn away, as tears flooded his eyes. He couldn't believe he was present to witness his mother and his sister at such a tender moment.

He would be present for all the moments in the future, he promised himself. He would soak up as much family time as he could.

CHAPTER 24

DECEMBER 31, 2007

Mae

That year, the Angel River Café started a new tradition and closed at noon on New Year's Eve so that Mae, her employees, and their families could enjoy a celebration in the early afternoon.

After conferring with Donaghy and Trina, Mae also decided to invite a few select members of her extended family to the party. Kate and Reed came by, of course. So did Susie and her son, Jack. Sharon arrived, still wearing her uniform, looking brashly beautiful and completely intimidating.

Ms. Maud from the library made an appearance, as did Mrs. Gruening from the Historical Society. Even Violet Morrow deigned to show up, bringing a large basket of healthy goodies from her store as a new year's gift. Mae winced when she saw a container of Brewer's Yeast in the basket, but she forced a smile and thanked Violet profusely.

After Levi had left town, Mae had decided that the time had come for her to face her fears, even those she felt were too silly and petty to require facing. One of the first things she'd done was find Violet and tell her the whole story of the book, how she'd given it to Levi to take to his mother, how consequently the town had been deprived of a treasure.

Violet had been stiff with displeasure at the news but on thinking it over had grudgingly admitted that Mae had made the right decision. "I might have done the same, in your place," she said. "That book belongs to Levi's mother as much as—or more than—it belongs to Angel River."

The concession may have been reluctant, but Mae embraced it for all it was worth, and she and Violet had been much closer in the days since.

The party was over by six. Trina and Donaghy had offered to help with the cleanup, but Mae shooed them away. "Go enjoy yourselves, young people," she said. "Be safe and have fun."

Donaghy had hugged her impulsively. "I'm so glad you moved here," he whispered. "I don't know what we would do without you."

And that was the best present that Mae could have hoped for.

Or so she thought at the time.

Mae finished the last of the cleanup and hung her apron on its hook. In her closet-sized office, she packed up her laptop and the week's receipts. She'd discovered that spread-sheets were more fun if she did them at home in front of a crackling fire, with Ruby nestled snugly at her side.

Mae was ready to head home. Nothing was keeping her here. And yet, she couldn't quite bring herself to leave. She stood in the doorway of her closet-sized office, leaning back against the jamb, drinking in the sight of her beloved café. Night had long fallen, but streetlights filtered through the drawn blinds, filling the space with a dim glow. Colors were muted, the air was pleasantly cool, and the good, clean smells of lemon cleanser and coffee still hung in the air.

From this angle, Mae could almost see the entire restaurant. She saw the corner of the kitchen where she had first discussed Browning Weidler with Trina and Donaghy. Through the pick-up window between the kitchen and dining room, she saw the spot at the counter where Violet had told her about the secret compartments inside her house. And if she tilted her head to the right, she could see the table where Levi had sat on that first morning, speaking words that had sparked a quest and kindled a flame that she'd thought had long died out.

Even if she never saw Levi again, she wouldn't change a moment about these past few weeks, and she would always be grateful for the warmth and excitement that he'd brought into her life.

She reached for her coat and heard a knock at the door. Not the front door, but the back door.

Mae's heart took a leap.

Of course, it could be anyone. It could be Donaghy, coming back because he'd forgotten something. It could be Violet, wanting to get a head start on day-old pastries. But somehow Mae knew exactly who was outside of that door, waiting for her to open it.

She moved around the corner from her office, grasped the knob, turned and pulled it wide. And there, on the other side of the threshold, stood a tall, dark, handsome stranger.

Only he wasn't a stranger anymore.

Mae's heart rose like a balloon, ready to fly with happiness into the starry sky.

"You came back," she said.

"Of course," Levi replied calmly. "I told you I would."

· · ·

SHE BROUGHT HIM INSIDE AND OFFERED TO MAKE COFFEE, BUT he waved her away and went to the coffee machine himself.

"You've made me a lot of coffee in the short time we've known each other," he told her. "It's time for me to start making it for you. Do you think you could handle that?"

"I think I could, with effort." Mae took a seat at one of the stools at the cooking island. "How's your mother?"

"Feeling better." He measured coffee grounds into the reservoir, and pushed the button to start it brewing. "Feeling stronger. Of course, we don't know how long we'll have with her, but then again, nobody does. She's at the hotel right now."

Mae blinked. "Which hotel?"

"The Angel River Hotel, of course," he said. "She's there with my sister, waiting for us."

"Us?" Mae repeated, too blissful to care if she sounded like an idiot.

"You and me," Levi said in a careful, quiet voice. He pulled two mugs out of the cabinet and set them on the counter in front of her. Then he reached down to take her hand. "Us."

"Us," Mae said again, breathing the word on an exhale.

He dropped the pretense of calmness and pulled her off the stool, into his arms. "You and me," he said again, more firmly this time. "I want us to be an us. Is that okay with you?"

She laughed, suddenly realizing there were tears in her eyes. "I think I could get used to it," she said. "But what about Wyoming? What about your family?"

"We've been talking about relocating, if the town will have us," he said.

"All of you?" Mae asked, delighted.

"All of us," he repeated. "And *us*," he added, stroking her cheek.

"I like the sound of that." She slid her arms around his neck. "I like the sound of all of it."

"Good," said Levi. "I'm going to take your advice and start doing the hard work of building a life I can be proud of. In fact, I'm thinking of opening a bookstore. This town could use one."

EPILOGUE

The Book of Forgotten Angels
By Browning Weidler

Last Bell

*J*onathan Strick and his daughter Dora returned to her mother's grave on the morning of the new year. The day was crisp and cold, with thin sunlight and air fogged by breath. And yet, they were warm in their hearts and at peace in their souls.

It had been exactly a year since Dora had lost her mother, and Jonathan his wife. How well he remembered sitting at the bedside of that sweet lady, feeling her small, cold hand in his. Her chest had risen ever so slightly as she'd taken her last breath, then fallen again to rise no more. Her departure from the earthly plane had plunged him into a despair from which he never thought to emerge.

And yet, all things have an end. Even sorrow. Even stories. And if the end of sorrow brings happiness anew, the end of one story is often the beginning of the next.

So it was with Jonathan and Dora, as they wiggled their toes in their new boots and pulled their warm wrappings closer around them. The ending of the story that Jonathan had written for his benefactor had brought the beginning of a new chapter for himself and his little daughter—another sweet lady, though the meagerness of her years belied the label.

It had been Dora who had shown him the grace of angels hidden behind the rough brows of ordinary folk. The blind man on the corner, who gave his old dog first crack at whatever morsel of food that came their way. The baker's wife, who put by enough bread to feed the poor orphans huddled in the alley. Even their benefactor himself, who could well afford charity of all kinds, had elevated himself by the kindness and gentility with which he had welcomed them into his home.

"You only have to look for angels to find them," Dora had reminded Jonathan gently.

And so it was. And so it had been. And so, indeed, it always would be.

His daughter had showed him the angels. And truly, they were all around.

The End

If you enjoyed this book, a positive review would mean the world to me. Like all authors, my books rely heavily on word of mouth to reach new readers. Plus, every review gives me a new perspective on the story. And if you loved this book, then it's yours as much as mine, and I hope you'll want to share it with your fellow book lovers.

AUTHOR'S NOTE

Hello again! Thank you so much for making it all the way through. What did you think of the book? You can always email me at misha@mishacrews.com to let me know.

If you'd like to spend some more time with Mae and Levi (and Ruby, of course!), you can find some extra chapters at this link: tinyurl.com/ForgottenAngelsExtra.

Okay, I promised you some background notes, didn't I? Well, the first thing I want to tell you is that Angel River and its surroundings have become so real and tangible in my imagination that for a while I was afraid I might be delusional. Of course, this is not uncommon for writers; we frequently talk to our characters and refer to them in everyday conversation as if they were real people, which can be confusing to our friends and family. So, as I said, I was just starting to think that I might need to take what used to be called a "rest cure," when I realized this: fantasy is part of my job as a writer. (You probably already knew that didn't you? Sigh. Readers are so smart.) At that point, I decided to stop fighting my figments, so to speak, and take the Nestea plunge into my own imagination. As a result, I've started a series of blog posts about Angel River, and if you're at all interested you can find those on my website: MishaCrews.com/AngelRiver.

(By the way, if you don't know what the Nestea plunge is, the phrase comes from a series of commercials in the 1970s which featured people falling backwards into water. You can find them online if you're curious; hope they give you a chuckle.)

Now, as for the characters, it might interest you to know that Abel Stein, Wendell Beaufort and Violet Morrow have more of a connection than has so far been written. In this book we learned that Abe and Wendell grew up together. Violet was also part of that generation, and she is, in fact, the sister of Lily, who is the girl that both Abe and Wendell were in love with. More will be told about their relationship in future novels.

And what about those hidden houses in the woods, where Levi visited Wendell—the Big Sister and the Little Sister? There will be at least one book set in those houses, starting with a novel called *Back of the Moon*, which will be book seven in the Angel River series, and should be out in summer of 2024.

Ha-la, the Dutch folklore that's mentioned in this book and also in *The House on the Hill*, is fictional. However, it's invention was inspired by a Pennsylvania Dutch folk practice called Powwow, which is still in use today.

Browning Weidler is also fictional, as I'm sure you guessed. Very little is known about him at this time (even by me). There's a rumor floating around that Browning Weidler may not even be his real name. We'll explore that more in future stories as well.

The next book in the Angel River series is called *Sweet Music*. Mae and Levi make an appearance, as do Kate and

Reed from *Homesong* and *The House on the Hill*. Josie Sullivan is desperate

I love hearing from readers, and I hope you will email me sometime at misha@mishacrews.com. You can also find me on my website, mishacrews.com, and all across social media @MishaCrews.

If you enjoyed this book and can spare the time, a positive review would be greatly appreciated. Like most authors, I depend on word-of-mouth recommendations to reach new readers. There's an enormous sea of reading material out there (for which we booklovers are very grateful) and one kind word from a reader like you can make the difference between whether this book sinks or swims. Thanks in advance!

And thank you again for reading. The next time I see you, we'll be enjoying some *Sweet Music* together.

ABOUT THE AUTHOR

Misha Crews is the bestselling author of multiple romantic novels and short stories. Readers have called her work "head and shoulders above the usual fare of contemporary romance novels," "absolutely fascinating," and "original." Born in Charlottesville, Virginia, Misha was raised near Washington, D.C., and now lives in the Shenandoah Valley, where she writes love stories about old houses and family secrets.

facebook.com/MishaCrewsAuthor
instagram.com/mishacrews
goodreads.com/mishacrews
pinterest.com/MishaCrews

ALSO BY MISHA CREWS

Angel River Novels

Homesong

The House on the Hill

The Book of Forgotten Angels

Sweet Music

Still Waters

A Bend in the River - Coming in 2024!

Short Fiction

At the Cafe and Other Stories

The Magic Hour

The Violet Hour

All I Want for Christmas is a Happy Halloween

Romantic Suspense

Her Secret Bodyguard